# The
# Center

# The Center

## From a Troubled Past to a New Life

CAROLYN MEYER

A MARGARET K. MCELDERRY BOOK

*Atheneum*      1980      *New York*

Library of Congress Cataloging in Publication Data
Meyer, Carolyn.
The Center: from a troubled past to a new life.

"A Margaret K. McElderry book."
SUMMARY: Describes the experiences of a troubled teenager at the
Vitam Center in Norwalk, Connecticut, therapeutic community where
teenagers with problems help each other get better.
1. Vitam Center—Juvenile literature.   2. Problem children—Services for
Connecticut—Norwalk—Juvenile literature.   [1. Vitam Center.
2. Emotional problems.   3. Rehabilitation of juvenile delinquents]
I. Title.
HV885.N9M49          362.7'4          79-12509
ISBN 0-689-50143-9

Copyright © 1979 by Carolyn Meyer
All rights reserved
Published simultaneously in Canada by McClelland & Stewart, Ltd.
Composed by American-Stratford Graphic Services, Inc.
Brattleboro, Vermont
Printed and bound by R. R. Donnelley & Sons
Crawfordsville, Indiana
Designed by Marjorie Zaum

First Printing August 1979
Second Printing May 1980

*for the Vitam Family,*
*and especially for John,*
*with love*

*The*
*Center*

CHAPTER I

*I won't stay. Don't worry about that. They can't force me. A month maybe. Then I'll be back.*

He had said it to Billy last night when they were crouching in the garage for one last joint. "They'll *make* you stay," Billy said. "They'll really mess up your head."

*No they won't. I won't let them.* He had felt sure of it last night, relaxed and mellow, with the reefer going back and forth between them. Now, with most of his clothes stuffed in two suitcases next to his unmade bed, he was trying hard to hang onto it. They said they'd bring his stereo and records later. He doubted they'd keep their word. They hadn't been known for that.

"David!"

He looked around his room; it was a pigsty. Let her clean it up. Always bitching about how messy he was. "Fifteen years old and you still can't hang up your clothes." Blah-blah-blah. Now he wouldn't be here any more. Who would she yell at now? Susie? Susie was as bad as he was, but she hardly ever got yelled at. Richie? Richie was perfect, Richie always made his own bed, Richie always put his dirty laundry in the hamper. They thought even his shit was perfect.

"David! It's time to go."

Both of them down there peeing their pants, so anxious to

3

take him away. The Center is not a jail, they had told him about seventeen times, or a nuthouse. It's a place where they help you. You won't be locked up or anything. You can leave any time you want to.

Bullshit. He didn't need help. Everything would be just fine if they'd leave him alone. They'd straighten him out, his father said. He didn't need straightening out. *Just get off my back!* If they gave him enough of an allowance, he wouldn't need to steal. Richie and Susie, all they had to do was ask, and it was handed over to them, whatever they wanted. But when *he* asked, forget it!

"David, come on! Your father's waiting."

*Let the bastard wait.* But he picked up the suitcases, kicked an overflowing ashtray under the bed, and walked out.

His father drove in silence. His mother, half turned around in the front seat, talked nonstop. "What a beautiful day!" she announced in that phony cheerful voice of hers. "Not too many more like this, I guess. The nights are already starting to get cool."

When she got done talking about the weather, she started in on things he had probably forgotten to pack. Toothpaste? Had he remembered that? Did he think he had enough underwear? If not, for goodness sake let her know. Socks too. On and on she went. He didn't listen to any of it. He had learned to tune it all out.

He sat in the back seat, staring at their heads. His father was practically bald. The top of his head was smooth and shiny. His mother had tried to get him to buy a wig. She dyed her hair. She said it wasn't really dyeing, just rinsing to cover the gray. It must be terrible to get old, he thought. Just to work and take care of kids and worry about money and stuff. Not to have fun like he did, getting high and riding around on Billy's motorcycle and partying all the time. They didn't do anything like

4

that. He wondered if they had ever tried pot. Probably not. Really square. Sometimes his father drank too much, though, and acted like a stupid kid. Once he saw his father kissing their next door neighbor, Mrs. Marinaro. He wondered what other stuff his father did.

It took them a half-hour to get there, and then his father almost missed the driveway because the blue sign with the white letters, THE CENTER, was nearly hidden by tree branches. His mother, who was still rattling away about God knows what, went into high gear. She said she thought the place must have been beautiful at one time. Just look at that old stone mansion and the Greek columns at the front door and those lovely big windows. Imagine what it must have been like to live there, acres and acres of land and all those trees and a pond down below. . . .

*It sucks. I won't stay.*

His father parked the car and picked up one of the suitcases. He still hadn't said anything. Probably mad because he had to take a few hours off from work to deliver David here, to make sure he didn't run away again, just take off for somewhere when it was time to go, maybe not come back for hours. He used to do that when they had an appointment with the shrink. Drove his mother crazy; she'd race all over town looking for him, never found him. When he came back she'd tell him he was grounded, couldn't leave the house for a million years and so on. He just laughed; at night he went out through his window, down over the porch roof, running all the way to Billy's.

They were both pretty dressed up. His mother had on the outfit she always wore when she wanted to make a good impression. He wondered what they would do when they left here without him. Maybe go out and celebrate. They were finally getting rid of him.

He set his teeth and followed his mother through the big

front door. He felt his gut tighten and his hands start to sweat. People were charging back and forth through the entrance hall, and a girl sitting at the desk lit up a big smile for them.

"Welcome to the Center. May I help you?"

She had blue eyes and long brown hair with flashes of red in it. Sensational tits that bounced when she went through a door to tell somebody the Petersons had arrived. While they waited for her to come back, he stared at a large sign over the door: HONESTY.

*Crap.*

They had been here before, a month ago, for the interview. His father had taken off from work that day, too. A guy with a beard, Doctor Somebody, had talked to him and asked him a lot of questions. Stupid questions: Do you like yourself? How do you think other people feel about you? Why do you think you are here? Questions about what drugs he'd been taking and how often, about how he was getting along in school. He gave the guy bullshit on the dumb questions, lied about the drugs, told him the truth about school. Actually the doc didn't seem too bad; no worse than any other adult, probably.

The doctor had explained how the Center worked, what it was like. It was a place where people helped each other to solve their problems, he said. It was a place where you could change and become a better person. There were about a hundred program members, three times more boys than girls, half of them staying at the Center, the rest living at home and coming in every day.

There were some rules he'd have to follow. No drugs. No violence. Those were the main ones. Some other stuff, too: he wouldn't be allowed to get in touch with negative people, with any of his old friends, by mail or by phone or in person.

Doc had said they all thought he would progress faster if

he moved into the dormitory. He would let them know as soon as they had a bed available, probably in a few weeks.

After the interview his mother had asked him what he thought.

It's okay, he had told her. If I have to go some place it might as well be there.

But he hadn't said what he really thought: *I won't stay*.

Then three days ago the call had come. He was being admitted to the program. There was a bed available for him.

"Good-bye, Davey. Good luck." His father stood impassively with his hands behind his back. His mother tried to give him a hug, but he held himself stiff and didn't hug her back. Then they turned and left, their heads lowered. There was a part of him that wanted to run after them. But another part, the tougher part, was glad to see them go: *I don't give a shit*.

Before the hot heavy stone in his gut could lurch again, somebody put a hand on his shoulder. Some guy with curly hair and a red beard. "You're David, right? I'm Kevin Murphy. Come on up to the office and let's talk."

He followed the red hair to a scruffy little room decorated with a few faded posters. Kevin flopped in a chair, angled his feet up on the battered desk, leaned back with his hands behind his head. "So tell me something about yourself, Dave."

"What do you want to know?" Sullen.

"Why you're here, for instance."

He shrugged and recited bits of the story. Not getting along with his parents, not getting along in school, shoplifting.

"You get high, too?"

He nodded.

"Using other stuff?"

He hesitated. Why should he tell this creep anything? Kevin picked up on the hesitation and helped him out. "Dave, listen,

7

I've been in exactly the spot you're in now. Maybe a worse one. I was trying everything they made, and I was a mess. Then I came here. You don't want to be here, right? I didn't want to be here either. I was a little older than you, and nobody was going to shut me up anywhere. But I came here, and eventually I got rid of all that shit. Not all at once. It took me more than two years, but I got rid of it. Now I'm working here as a counselor."

At this place for two years and now he's working here? *Not me! I'm not staying.* . . .

But gradually David felt the stone in his stomach soften. For a little while he forgot about it. This guy Kevin had really been there too, knew more about how David was feeling than maybe he knew about himself. And that idea scared him. The whole place was beginning to scare him.

Kevin explained that David was now a member of the Orientation part of the program. For the next few months, as long as he was in OR, Kevin would be his primary counselor. They'd get together alone a couple of times a week, and David would be in groups also, and eventually he'd get to know all the other ORs and the Intermediates and some of the Phase-Outs, plus most of the counselors and the guys at the top, like Paul Kendricks, the program director, and George Miller, the clinical director, and Dr. Stone, the psychiatrist, and some others—the high rollers, as everybody called them.

*Like hell I will.*

After a while Kevin took him downstairs and introduced him to a kid all duded up in a flashy green necktie. The kid, Jay Bailey, started right in on him while they were walking up the hill toward the Greenhouse, the men's dorm. "So how come you're here?"

David told him. "How long you been here?"

"Eleven months," Jay said. "I'm an Intermediate."

"You ever feel like leaving?"

"Lots of times. Everybody does."

"You ever do it?"

"Once. For three days. Then I came back."

"What'd they do when you came back?"

"Put me on the chair for a couple of days. Gave me a General Meeting. Cut my hair."

*"They cut your hair?"*

"Yeah. That's what they do when you break one of the cardinal rules. You'll see. Happens all the time. I still think about leaving sometimes."

*I won't stay. . . .*

Jay showed him around the dormitory, took him to a room with bunk beds, showed him where to put his clothes. "Time for Morning Meeting," Jay told him on the way back down to the main house.

*"Morning* meeting? It's the middle of the afternoon."

"That's because we wait for everybody to come back from school. When there's no school, we have it in the morning."

"So why don't you call it Afternoon Meeting?"

"Because it's always been Morning Meeting."

They found seats in the dining room. In a few minutes Kevin came in with a tall black man and a beautiful woman with a great fountain of blond hair. Hands popped up like daisies in answer to some unasked question, and the black man pointed to one of them. Fists shoved in the pockets of his jeans, the boy stood in front of the group. "Good afternoon, family."

The family murmured back, and the boy rattled through something that David couldn't quite catch—a sort of a prayer or something about troubles and honesty and trust and love.

"Thank you, Tim."

The black man began to read names from a sheet, and one by one the people named got up and addressed the group. Who left the soda can outside the front door? Who broke the shelf in the bathroom? Who's been pulling the stuffing out of the sofa cushions in the men's dormitory? Yeah, well, I guess that was me. You *guess?* You don't *know?* Okay, yeah, I did it. So it's about time you get over pulling dumb shit like that. A lot of people around here better start improving their attitudes.

*What a bunch of creeps.* Every little thing.

A baby-faced boy waved his hand. "Can I make a pull-up?"

"Is your name on the pull-up sheet, Bryan?"

"I didn't have time."

"You know the rules. Next time. Anybody got any announcements?"

Hands waved again. A thin girl in a fuzzy yellow sweater that made her look like a scrawny chicken stood up. "I want to talk to people about having feelings about leaving and getting high."

Murmurs of "All right, Patty."

"I want to be talking to people about being honest," a boy said.

*God, how ridiculous can you get?*

Then the black man asked, "Anybody got any entertainment?" Grinning self-consciously, Jay motioned to a few of his friends, and eventually four of them were standing up front, shifting from foot to foot. After a few false starts they sang a song, pretty much off-key. Everybody clapped and the black man whistled through his teeth and said maybe they ought to run through it a few more times before they took it on the road.

"There's going to be a couple of groups this afternoon," Kevin announced and read off a list of names. Jay's name was on the list. David's was not. He felt relieved in a way, but he also wondered what was going to happen to him instead. Before Jay left for his group he said, "Don't worry. Lots of people be around to talk to you."

And there were. One kid after another came up to him, asking him his name, asking why he was there, telling him something about themselves. They all seemed like pretty good kids. He even liked them, in fact. He figured they must all be here because they had to be. He asked, "How come you don't leave?"

A few told him, "I been paroled here. If I wasn't here I'd be out at Starkweather." David knew about Starkweather, the state-operated school for delinquents.

Some of them had already done time there, and they told him about that, too. "Man, it's a lot easier out there than it is here. You learn your way around, you can slide through easy. Your time is up, you get out, but you're sure no better than when you went in and probably a whole lot worse. Here you can change. You can get a lot better."

David could see no reason to change. Yeah, so he had messed up a few times, had made a few stupid mistakes. But he could fix that on his own: get smarter, be more careful. And be free, getting high, running around with his friends. *I won't stay!*

David thought he had never talked so much, or been talked to so much, in his entire life. He was getting sick of it. He wanted to go up to his dormitory room and relax for a while, lie on his bunk and maybe look at a magazine or something. He started out the front door. Another kid in a necktie (*What's with all these neckties?*) stopped him. "Where you going?" He told him, up to read for a while. The kid shook his head. "Not unless staff says so. You're supposed to be here talking to people, getting to know people. Anyway, supper will be coming out soon."

Supper? It was barely four-thirty.

But in the dining room everyone was sitting around at the tables. The boy in the necktie steered him to an empty chair. He hadn't seen any of them before, except the girl. It was the one with the beautiful tits. "New member," the boy said. "Pull him in."

And while they waited for their turn in the food line, they

went over the same damn thing again, about how he could change here, and so on. Finally a guy with a clipboard called their table and they joined a short line at a counter outside the kitchen. Kids wearing white paper hats dished out spaghetti, meatballs, sauce, bread, beans. They helped themselves to salad, canned peaches, cookies, milk from a cooler.

While they ate, the conversation worked around to other things, other subjects besides who David Peterson was and why he was at the Center. He listened absentmindedly, said little. He could hardly take his eyes off those tits.

The meal over, the clean-up crew urged those who were finished eating to leave the dining room so they could do the floors. David drifted toward the living room and sank down onto the sofa between two girls. One of them, a fat, pimply girl, said, "You're new here, right? Well, you're not supposed to sit down between two girls. You got to trade places with one of us." Another rule! He made the switch.

A boy appeared in the doorway. "David Peterson?"

"Here!"

"You're wanted in the front office."

*What now?* David followed the boy to a small office next to the main hall. Two staff members he'd seen but hadn't met were eating from trays at the desks. One of them was a huge burly man with thick yellow hair and beard. "Hi, you David Peterson? I'm Paul Kendricks." He had a deep, gravelly voice. They shook hands. "Okay, I know you're new here and you don't know the rules yet, but I want to explain something to you. We got a lot of guys here and a lot of girls, and we live pretty close together. Now, the only way we can handle all that togetherness is if we treat each other like brothers and sisters. You get what I mean? That means there's no sex. You don't fuck, you don't touch, you don't even *look* at her in a certain way. You understand that? Now Valerie—the girl you ate supper with tonight—Valerie says you spent the whole time staring at her boobs. Is that true?"

Embarrassed! What the hell? Who was this jerk to tell him what he could look at and what he couldn't? "No."

"No? You're saying you weren't staring at her tits?"

"No, I wasn't. I didn't even notice them."

"That's bullshit, man! How could you help but notice them! She came in here and told me you were staring. You say you weren't. Valerie has been in the program for a year and has learned something about being honest. You've been here for a couple of hours, and you're showing me right now you have a lot to learn. So I *know* you're lying, and *you* know I know you're lying. The rule is that you don't look at the girls here in a sexual way. I know that's hard to do, and it's normal to want to, but you have to learn to control it. What's more important is that you start right now learning to be honest—with yourself, with everybody else here. Okay, you got that?"

David nodded dumbly, humiliated.

"Okay, get out of here now."

David stumbled away, angry—at Paul Kendricks, at Valerie, at himself. He managed to sit by himself in a corner of the living room. He thought he couldn't stand another of those conversations that allowed him no secrets. For a while nobody bothered him. People hurried in and out. One of the boys had a broom and was laboriously sweeping the carpets. Someone stuck his head in and requested that nobody go through the lobby while they were mopping the floor. The cleaning seemed endless and obsessive. David hoped that nobody had any ideas about him doing this kind of crud work. He thought of the mess he had left in his room at home that his mother would have to clean up.

"Intermediates in the dining room!"

About half the people who had been lounging around in the living room got up and left, and the rest moved closer together. A girl with long blonde hair bent forward as she combed it, a shining waterfall, then flipped it back over her head. Moments later she combed it forward again. A boy named Felipe with a Spanish accent and a hazy mustache demonstrated an elaborate way to lace his sneakers. A hefty girl in carpenter's jeans, chewing the end of a strand of dull hair, announced in a whiny voice that she was thinking of splitting. Immediately the silly conversations stopped and everyone turned to the girl. "I don't have to stay here," she said. "I can go to Starkweather."

"Hey, Rosalie, you ever *been* to Starkweather?"

"No."

"Well, I been there, and I can tell you this is better."

"Staff know you're thinking about leaving?"

"Yeah, I told Yvonne today."

"So what'd she say?"

"She got me to accept this contract that I'd stay until my thirty days are up, and then I can decide if I want to go or not."

"So how many days you got?"

"Thirteen."

"Then you better just stop talking about going and think about saying for the next thirteen days. That's not keeping the contract if you're talking about going all the time."

"I don't care! I'm sick of being here! I'm sick of talking all the time, and all the rules and everything."

"You think they got no rules at Starkweather? Ha!"

"Yeah, but not like here."

"Look, Rosalie, you got to be somewhere, right? If you got to be somewhere, then this is the best place to be."

One of them turned to David suddenly. "How you like it here so far?"

"It's okay, I guess. If you got to be somewhere. . . ."

They laughed at his little joke and it made him feel better.

Kevin strolled in, thumbs hooked in his belt loops. "Yo, what's happening?"

"Kevin, you got time to talk?"

"Not now, Chris, we're going to do something here. All you OR's, how about moving some furniture around so we got a circle, and then we'll try a game and see how it goes."

David helped them shift the heavy sofa; another boy brought in some folding chairs from the dining room. The Intermediate. meeting had ended, and most of the Intermediates had gone off to group sessions.

"How many of you ever played this game? You start with one person—how about you, Rosalie?—and you say, 'I'm going on a trip and I'm going to take, blank,' and then you mention something you're going to take. And then the next person says, 'I'm going on a trip and I'm going to take' whatever Rosalie said and then adds something new. We go around the circle and each person tries to name all the things the person before said, in order, plus something new. Okay? Questions? Rosalie, why don't you start."

Rosalie, grumpy, began the round, naming a pack of cigarettes. Felipe added shoelaces. Carla, the girl with the long blonde hair, said, "I'm going on a trip and I'm going to take a pack of cigarettes, shoelaces, and a comb." But the next kid got confused and missed; soon it was David's turn. He was annoyed to find himself getting tense over such a stupid game, but he named off the list and added a rock record to the baggage. There were eighteen people in the circle at the start. Five dropped out on the first round. By the fourth round the list was long and complicated, and only six people remained. Hands sweating, David struggled to stay in the game. The girl with the blonde hair dropped out, and then three more, until it was just fat Rosalie and himself.

"You're the winners!" Kevin announced. "Congratulations, Rosalie and David!"

Everyone clapped. Rosalie beamed. David couldn't believe it, couldn't remember the last time he had won any kind of a game or contest. Flushed and embarrassed, he followed the others into the dining room where cookies and milk had been set out for a late snack. Intermediates were drifting down from the upstairs rooms where their encounter groups had met. A couple of the boys looked as though they had been crying, their eyes red and puffy. Boys crying? David couldn't imagine what went on in those groups, but he knew one thing: *They'll never see me cry.*

Suddenly he was very tired. But it wasn't over yet. They were making the house tight, cleaning it one more time before everybody went home or to their rooms. A few cars had pulled up in the driveway outside; parents coming in to pick up kids who lived at home. He wondered how he would feel if he were going home. He knew what it would be like: his father asking nothing, saying nothing; his mother trying to drag out of him a full report of everything that had happened all day. It was a relief to be staying.

Then Eddie, his roommate, came looking for him. David couldn't figure why they were putting him in with this babyish kid who looked about twelve years old and had a speech defect that made him pronounce things funny. David didn't like him. He didn't know why. But he followed him silently up the hill to the Greenhouse. David dug out the new pajamas his mother had packed for him and put them on. Eddie watched him. "You take a shower?"

"No."

"Well, you gotta take one. It's a rule here." He pronounced the r like a w: *wule.*

Furious, David raced into the shower room, rinsed quickly,

pulled his pajamas back on over his damp skin. Trotting back down the hall, he saw that a couple of guys had settled down in their rooms to do their homework. Somebody had turned on the television in the lounge, but he was too exhausted to watch.

He was in his bunk before lights-out at eleven, aching for sleep. Up through the weariness came the first rush of fear and anxiety and hurt that had been bottled up in him all day. David kept his face muffled in his pillow and struggled for control. Then he heard Eddie's voice in the bunk below him. "It's okay to cry. Everybody does here. You got to let it out."

David let go in great heaving gasps. Then finally he slept.

Mr. and Mrs. Peterson drove home in silence.

"What do you think?" Mrs. Peterson asked, twisting her wedding ring around and around her finger.

"I suppose it's as good a place as any," Mr. Peterson replied, turning into the driveway of a white house with dark green shutters. "We'll see."

The Petersons lived on a street lined with many similar houses, their lawn regularly mowed and the shrubbery neatly trimmed like all the others. Richard Peterson noticed that the house needed a paint job. He would have to do it himself, since he couldn't afford now to hire someone. All that money paid out for psychiatrists and psychologists and God knew who else for David, and nothing they did seemed to help. When David first started getting into trouble, he and Ellen had argued about him a lot. Their older son, Richie, had never been a problem. A senior in high school, he got good grades and planned to go to the state university next year. And Susie was a sweetheart, already twelve but still cute and bouncy and loving. Richard Peterson hoped she would always stay that way: his little Susie Pie.

Funny how it had all worked out. Young Richard, his name-sake, had trailed after him all the time when he was a little kid, helping him around the yard, always going to get his tool set to fix things when Richard was working on a project around the house. Richie had always obeyed. Richard had made it clear that he believed in discipline and obedience. A kid did what you told him to do, and if he didn't you let him have it. You let him know who was in charge. He remembered his own father taking off his belt and walloping him once in a while, and it certainly hadn't done any harm. After a few times all his father had needed to do was to start unbuckling and Richard had straightened out right away. Richard had done the same thing with young Richie, and with the same results. A few good lickings when he was still young enough to learn the lesson, and after that there had been no serious problems. Richie was growing up to be like him: serious, hard-working, able to take it.

Susie had been handled differently, of course. The girl they wanted so much after two boys, blonde, blue-eyed, looking just like her mother, climbing up on his lap, snuggling up to him, saying, "Daddy, I love you." The boys had never done that. He couldn't remember David ever climbing up on his lap or snuggling or saying anything about loving him. It occurred to him that he probably let Susie get away with murder. But when he yelled at her, or even spoke sharply to her, she got this awful stricken look on her face, and the tears started to wind down her cheeks and he just couldn't punish her. He never could.

But David! David had been a rebel, it seemed to his father, almost from the minute he was born. Not at all like the other two. Richie looked just like his father and acted like him too. Susie was a carbon copy of her mother. But David didn't look like either of them, and he didn't seem to act like them either. Richard was ashamed to admit it, but there had been times, especially lately, when he had allowed himself to ponder the secret thought that had wormed its way into his mind: maybe David was not his own son. For a long time he had refused even to admit the thought existed. But surely no son of his, no one of his blood, could ever act like this!

For a while he had actually wondered if somehow the babies had been switched in the hospital nursery. Once he had even asked his wife about it. She had been a nurse for a long time; she'd have some idea. He had been careful how he brought up the subject, never of course mentioning his thoughts about David. "Ever hear of anything happening like that over at Holy Cross? Babies switched?" But she had laughed at him. A one-in-a-million chance; there were too many safeguards. When he had pressed her—"But it *could* happen, couldn't it? It's not completely impossible?"—she had given him that peculiar look, as though she might have known what he was thinking, and he had dropped the subject.

But there was another possibility, and that one was not such a long shot in Richard's mind. David had been conceived at a rocky time in their marriage. Richard had been out of work for a while, the company he had worked for had let him go, and Ellen had gone back to general duty nursing. On the bottom of the seniority list, she had worked all kinds of crazy hours, night shifts, weekends, whatever they had given her. He had been hard to get along with then, he realized. What man would not be? Dependent on his wife's paycheck, home all day with a little kid —Richie was only fifteen months old—while she was meeting all those handsome, rich doctors at the hospital, men with more money and prestige than he would ever have. He had worried about it at the time, but of course he had never said anything. He had forgotten about it, in fact, because by the time she was four months pregnant with David he had had another job—a good one, and he had gone right up in the company—and he had made her quit and stay home, even though she had argued that she liked nursing and there was plenty of chance for her to get private duty work every now and then. It would have helped out in paying for the house they wanted to buy, and besides she said she needed to keep her hand in, to keep her skills from getting rusty. But he had put his foot down. He earned the money and paid the bills; she took care of the house and kids. She might have been a little unhappy at first, but she had never mentioned it again. And then Susie had come along.

After that they had been happy for a long time. But right from the beginning, as Richard Peterson looked back on it, there had been something different about David. When Richard had tried to punish it out of him, the boy had become even wilder. And his mother had always stepped in to try to protect him, as though he was somebody special. Things had seemed to get worse as the years went by. He would tell David one thing, she'd tell him something else. Once, in his fury at the boy, he had struck out at her. In his anger she had seemed to him to be the same person as David. He had felt horrible afterward, had apologized, had done everything he could to make it up to her. But after that she had seemed to grow cold to him.

Maybe David was really a doctor's son. It had driven Richard nearly insane to think of it. But then he had calmed down, and Susie would come and curl up in his lap, or Richie would bring him a good report card or make the track team. Richard Peterson thought to himself: *Two out of three—that's not a bad average in this day and age.*

Ellen Peterson lay on the far edge of the bed and allowed the tears to drip off her nose and run onto the pillow. Her husband had not yet begun to snore; therefore he must still be awake. She wondered what he was thinking about. There was no point in asking, because she knew he would never tell her.

And she wasn't sure she'd know what to say if he ever did tell her how he felt.

This business with David was the worst thing she could think of that she had ever had to go through. Nothing else that could happen to her would affect her like this.

David was the child who needed her most. He always had been. A restless, colicky baby from the very begining, he had been born at a time when she wondered if her marriage would survive. Richard had been out of a job, there wasn't much money, he had resented her working. But she had loved it. The hours were awful, but she enjoyed being out of the house every day. She had liked the patients, liked the feeling that she was really helping people, liked having a paycheck. She had a couple of good friends on the staff, and sometimes they went out to eat when they came off their shift. Occasionally some of the young residents had gone along. One of them had even asked her to go for a drink with him. She had refused, but when she got home, tired but exhilarated after a demanding day, Richard was sullen and accusing as though he knew she had been asked but didn't know she had refused. About that time she got pregnant. She didn't want another child right then, but Richard had insisted. He said he thought Richie needed company, but she knew he wanted it as a reason to keep her at home again. But then when the baby had been born, something had happened. He had seemed to resent David. She didn't know why, and she couldn't ask.

David had always been a handful. She didn't think Richard's authoritarian attitude was at all necessary, but she couldn't argue with the fact that Richie was a beautifully behaved child. David wasn't. The worse he acted, the harder Richard came down on him. David had a way of driving Richard into a fury, and eventually he struck her, too. When he did that, something died inside her. Sometimes she thought of leaving him, but she knew she could never do that. She would not know how to survive. It scared her. And in the meantime, she had another child. Pretty Susie, who looked exactly like her own baby pictures.

David had been in sixth grade when he brought home the first D on his report card. Richard had raised the roof, taking away all kinds of privileges until his grades went back up again. But it hadn't worked. She had known he was not coming straight home from school, and when he did go to his room he certainly wasn't doing his homework. She had felt like a jailer, because Richard had made it clear it was her responsibility to see that David straightened out. Richard obviously couldn't do that and go out and earn a living, too. It was her job, and she had hated it.

The grades had gotten worse. David had refused to do anything around the house. He was hardly ever home. They seemed to have fought constantly. He screamed obscenities at her, disappeared for hours at a time. She heard herself yelling things at him she had never imagined herself saying. It had been a nightmare from which she never woke up.

One day a year ago she had looked out the window and seen a police car with the revolving blue light. A man who identified himself as a detective with the juvenile division asked if David was at home. She had to say that she didn't know where he was, that he hadn't come home from school yet. He told her he was investigating a claim that someone in the neighborhood had been breaking into mailboxes and stealing from them. A federal offense. He hated to have to say it, but there was certain evidence . . . was it possible that David . . . ?

Aching, sick in her stomach, she admitted that it was possible, and she prayed that it would not be.

It had started the previous winter, the detective told her. People had realized that things were missing from their mailboxes —merchandise that had been ordered, magazines that usually arrived regularly. The post office had investigated. Then someone in the neighborhood reported seeing a boy who answered David's description rifling a box.

The detective had apologized. He was sorry to upset her, but there was nothing else he could do. She had said she understood. He said he would continue his investigation and be back in touch with her. He really needed to speak with David. At last he had left.

Heart pounding, Ellen had climbed the stairs to David's room. It was a mess. This was one of the things she and Richard argued about. He wanted her to stand over David every day to make sure the room was clean, the bed made, the clothes picked up. Richie did it on his own. Susie was messy, but not like this. She had tried, but it took all her energy and nothing was accomplished. And she had sworn she would not set foot in it again.

But she had. She had plowed through the litter on the floor, the piles of clothes and dirty dishes and caches of stale, spoiled food. Cigarette butts were everywhere, even though they had forbidden him to smoke, at least in the house. Then she had found the magazines addressed to a family she did not know, on a street three blocks away, and a bankbook in that family's name. She had felt as though she were going to faint. A fat red piggy bank sat on a shelf; she opened it and pulled out a wad of singles, fives, tens. She thought of the times she believed money had been missing from her own wallet but hadn't been sure. Then she had found the box of bright-colored pills that she recognized instantly: amphetamines and barbiturates. An empty vitamin capsule bottle was partly filled with dried leaves of some sort that resembled oregano. Numb with shock, she had collected it all—

the money, the bankbook, the drugs—and taken them to her room. She had shoved everything in her bureau drawer and lay on the bed, unable to cry, to think, to feel anything but a roaring turbulence in her head, until she had heard Richard's car in the driveway.

Then it had begun. The detective, the probation officer, the school guidance counselor, the judge, the social worker, the psychiatrist. All of them had gotten in on it, and nothing had improved. Susie was constantly whining or on the verge of tears. Richie had become remote and withdrawn. He didn't want to hear anything about it. She had tried to talk to Richard, who said he hoped they'd lock David up and throw away the key. But they hadn't. Six months' probation, that was all. David had gotten worse. Richard blamed Ellen for protecting him. He had been furious—at David, at her. Then one of Ellen's friends, a psychiatric nurse at Holy Cross, had told them about the Center.

Today, then, it had seemed as though the nightmare might be ending. For the first time in months, Ellen Peterson had not dreaded waking up in the morning, had not wondered each time the phone rang if it would be something about David—the guidance counselor or assistant principal at school to say he was truant again, the manager of the discount store on the main shopping mall to say David had stolen some items and was being held in his office. She remembered David's whispered calls to his friends, the time she had gotten up late at night to go to the bathroom and had seen him drop lightly off the garage roof, climb on back of somebody's motorcycle, and coast silently down their driveway. Now all that had ended. He was in a safe place, and they'd help him get well. She could relax now, pay attention to her other two children, her husband, her home. It was all right now. But why did she still have this cold, metallic feeling in her stomach? It was a matter of time, she'd assured herself; it would take at least a few weeks to start feeling normal again. She was exhausted; they all were. But the tears kept running down her nose, and it was a long time before she fell asleep.

Door locked, window open, Richie Peterson stared at the rising September moon, headphones piping acid rock directly into his brain, and dragged the last couple of tokes from a roach. He was relaxed and mellow as he was every night when he locked himself in his room and smoked and listened to music. No pressures then. He thought about David, off in some kind of a loony bin, because he was too dumb to stay clear of trouble. Poor Dave! Richie wondered what had happened to him. He thought of his mother and how sad and miserable she had looked for months now. Maybe her life would be easier. Richie shifted uneasily and thought of his father, stern, showing no emotion, reminding Richie it was up to him to carry on the family name, to be somebody, to make something of himself. Susie was his favorite, but it was different with her; she was a girl.

I have to make it, Richie thought. But what's he going to say when my grades come back this marking period. They haven't been that terrific; not as good as they used to be. Might even fail math. That will kill him! Math was always his best subject, and he thinks it's supposed to be mine. God, I hate the damned stuff. When I tell him I want to be a carpenter, he just laughs at me. He wants me to be an accountant, go the whole route, a CPA, not just a bookkeeper like him. He wants me to have all the advantages he never had. "Be a success." What a crock of shit!

The record ended. There was nothing left of the roach. Hungry and thirsty, Richie padded softly downstairs through the darkened house to find something to eat.

Under a ruffled canopy, Susie turned restlessly in troubled dreams, and one of her stuffed animals fell softly to the floor.

* * *

Kevin Murphy collected his gear from the back seat of his Volkswagen and unlocked the door of the tiny cottage he had rented from an elderly widow. In exchange for a lowered rent, he took care of Hansel, the widow's enormous German shepherd, did a little yard work in the summer, kept the snow shoveled in the winter. The rent was still more than he could really afford; most people who worked at the Center shared apartments with somebody else. He had tried that for a while, but he liked his privacy, or as much as the widow would allow. When the weather was good, she was always at the kitchen window, a fat, deep-voiced woman who liked to kid him about his Brooklyn accent and his red beard. He knew that she lay in her bedroom facing his cottage and listened for his car to come in at night, and sometimes she was waiting for him when he came out in the morning. She tried to mother him from that window. It annoyed him and amused him. She was very much interested in his life. He told her about his kids at the Center and about his courses at the university, where he was still struggling, at the age of twenty-five, to get his bachelor's degree.

He put a John Coltrane record on the stereo, opened a can of beer, and flopped onto the bed to read his mail. There was a note from a girl in New Jersey, a schoolteacher, inviting him out for a weekend. He checked his calendar; he had to work at the Center on one of the days she wanted him to come. He debated whether to switch with somebody or to see if another weekend would suit her just as well. Or to forget the whole thing. He knew that she wanted to get seriously involved. But he did not. Of all the girls he had met in the last few years—the teacher in New Jersey, a couple of students at the university, and so on—the only one who really appealed to him was also a counselor at the Center, Betsy Coleman.

But he had done nothing about it. There was a strict rule

to keep the whole program from breaking down into a sexual free-for-all that everyone must regard everyone else as a brother or sister. That went for the staff, too. Once in the past, two counselors had become involved, and all hell had broken loose. They had gone to their supervisors, asking permission to date. Permission had been denied. If you told the kids they couldn't do something, you couldn't turn around and make different rules for the counselors. But that hadn't stopped his feelings. He decided to accept the invitation to go to New Jersey, if he could find somebody to trade days off with him.

Meanwhile, he had a paper due for a class in child development and another in the sociology of the family. He was tired of trying to do two things at once, but there seemed no other way. He couldn't save enough money to quit and go to school full time; he was barely scraping through as it was. At least there was no lack of material. He always used his own cases for his class work. The new kid, Peterson, who had arrived today, was a classic. Old man was a hard-ass, mother was too soft on him, kid was probably basically okay with a hell of a lot of things to deal with.

Kevin wondered if David would make it. He had been working in the Orientation part of the program for three years, ever since he had joined the staff. The kids all came into OR scared to death and acting like a bunch of tough guys to cover up. They were pretty careful who they took into the program—no violent or suicidal types, no severely retarded kids—picking as well as they could the kind of kid who seemed to have a chance of making it. For the first thirty days it was touch and go; you just didn't make any bets on who would stay or who would split. Kevin tried not to let himself get too deeply involved with a kid until that first month had gone by. He did what he could, watched, listened, talked, told the kid his own story, kept his fingers crossed.

But then he started getting really involved. He was the

primary counselor for ten kids, but he made it his business to get to know the other ORs too, and to keep in touch with them after they made Intermediates and Phase-Out. It was no easy nine-to-five job; conferences with other OR counselors, general staff meetings, encounter groups, individual counseling sessions, meetings with the parents, plus all the paperwork. And he tried to spend as much time as he could on the floor with the kids, eating with them in the dining room, taking some of the boys out to play soccer once in a while. If you did enough of that, you were hooked on any kid.

Kevin read a couple of chapters in his textbook for his class tomorrow night and decided to go to bed early. He was due at the Center at six forty-five in the morning for the wake-up. Everybody hated that shift. He turned out his light and thought again of the face of David Peterson: the long brown hair, the square jaw clamped tight, the blue eyes that would never quite look at his, the fingernails bitten down to the quick, the I-don't-give-a-shit slouch. But before he went to sleep he thought of Betsy Coleman, and he was too tired to banish her from his mind.

CHAPTER 2

TWELVE FOLDING METAL CHAIRS WERE JAMMED IN A TIGHT circle in the space between the desk and the file cabinets. It was too hot, and somebody opened the window. Then it was too cold, and somebody closed it again. They shifted restlessly until Kevin came in and took the last chair in the circle. "Anybody got anything?"

"Yeah, I do," said Patty, the skinny girl who wore her fuzzy sweater almost every day. She motioned to one of the boys to change seats with her so she could sit opposite Carla, a fragile-looking girl with hair so straight it looked as though it had been pressed with an iron. "How come you hang around Eddie Simmons all the time?" Patty flung at her. "You got eyes for him, or what?"

Carla was silent, eyes down, face half-hidden by the curtain of hair. She shook her head.

But Eddie Simmons was there, too—David's roommate with the speech defect—and Eddie confronted the silent girl too. Was she setting it up so she could be around him more than she had to be? When they worked together on the communications crew, wasn't it true that she hung around him a lot? Was she having thoughts about him?

The accusations became more intense, but Carla just shook her head. Practically everyone in the group was yelling at her angrily. Their irritation and chagrin at her, not so much for what she had been doing but for refusing to admit that she had been doing it, had been rising higher and higher. The loud anger hurt David's ears, but Kevin did not intervene. Then David saw the slow, silent tears begin on Carla's pale face.

"So what are you crying for?" someone demanded. Finally she shook back her hair and admitted what they all knew: she did sometimes have thoughts about Eddie. She did have eyes for him and flirted with him even though she knew it was wrong.

"Then why do you do it? Because flirting with some guy is the only way you can feel good about yourself? When you know it's against the rules? So how come you do it then?"

Sobbing now, eyes unattractively puffy and china-white skin

turning blotchy, Carla began to relate—to let them know what it was like to be inside Carla's head. The mood of the group changed immediately.

"Let it out," they coaxed her. "Tell us how you feel."

Bit by bit, she told them. How before she had come to the Center, she had had lots of guys. The only way she knew to be friends with a guy was to go to bed with him; that was how she knew he liked her. There had been a lot of them. She didn't know how many. And she still thought of that, sometimes wished she were outside again, doing those things.

"But how did it make you feel when you were doing that, Carla?"

"It made me feel cheap." She sobbed. Someone passed a box of tissues from the desk, and Carla blew her nose and dabbed at her eyes.

"So now you feel like the only way you can get good feelings about yourself is to flirt? Even though you know it's wrong?"

"I know. But sometimes I can't help it."

Kevin interrupted gently. "Look, Carla, these feelings are natural. Everybody has them. But we're telling you to control them, not to set yourself and somebody else up for them. But if you're not being honest, with yourself and with us, then we can't help you. You understand that?" A silent nod. "How long you been in the program now, Carla?" Three months. "That's long enough to know. Long enough to have learned something about honesty, right?" Carla nodded again. There was a moment of quiet, the tension was relaxed.

But not for long. "What about you, Dave? What have you been up to?"

He had been expecting it sometime, but not right then, and he retreated. "Nothing."

"Don't give me 'nothing'!" Kevin warned him. "You and

Tony, there, up to 'nothing' down in the laundry room? What's the story? And sit up, please. This isn't afternoon nap time."

David flashed a look at Tony Russo and knew he was in for a bad time.

The arrival of Tony two weeks ago had been a shock. They used to hang out together, get high together, and a couple of times they had relieved EconoMart of a few items, such as an expensive watch for Tony's sister's birthday. Tony had hardly gotten in the door of the Center when he had come tearing over to greet David like a long-lost brother. It was a stupid thing to do.

"You two know each other?"

There had been no point in lying; it was obvious they did. And it was the big guy with the yellow beard who had caught them. "Get this," he told them. "Another rule: new program members never hang around each other, and especially new program members who are old friends. Can you guess why?"

They had shaken their heads. It seemed like a dumb rule. They could keep each other from getting homesick.

Paul Kendricks had explained. "Because new members are almost always negative. What you both need is to be around older members, so you can learn something about what's going on here, learn something about yourself. You two ever get into trouble together?"

Tony had started to deny it, but David had known it was no use. Paul had an uncanny sense of when you were lying. "Yeah," David had said. "A couple of times."

"A *couple* of times! I have a pretty good feeling it was a *lot* of times. So I'm going to put you two on the ban. That means you don't talk together, you don't look at each other, period. It's just like you don't exist as far as the other one is concerned. And you both get busy getting to know older members, people who can do you some *good*."

But this morning they had seen each other in the basement laundry room. Who had broken the ban? Afterwards David admitted he had. But it was definitely Tony who had proposed the negative contract.

"You probated here?" Tony had whispered.

"No. My parents made me come."

"You're not going to stay, are you?"

"I don't know. I been here five weeks. I figure I'll stick around awhile longer. People here are okay. It's gettin' high I miss."

"You tried to get any grass here? Pills? Anything?"

"I haven't seen any, and you got to be careful who you ask or you get killed."

"Listen," Tony said, "if you get hold of any, you let me in on it, and if I find any, I'll do the same for you. That a deal?"

They had been about to give their special handshake when Jay Bailey, wearing that ugly green necktie, had appeared in the doorway. "I thought you guys were on the ban."

"We are."

"Then you got no business down here together. One of you got to leave until the other one is finished."

Tony had nodded. "I'll go."

But minutes later they had been together in the front office, being blown away by Paul Kendricks. "What kind of a pair of dumb assholes are you?" he had roared at them. "I told you you're on the ban. You're not supposed to talk to each other, right? So what kind of crap were you two cooking up down there in the laundry room? Any negative contracts? Gettin' high together, maybe splitting together, anything like that?"

David had felt the blood rising, pounding in his head as Paul bellowed. He hadn't been able to face Paul and had kept his eyes on the floor. They had shaken their heads, but David had known it was far from over.

"So what's the story?" Kevin was insisting in a hard, sharp voice, and the rest of the group waited. David struggled to find an answer for him, something that would not make matters worse. They had never really been on his case too hard in his five weeks here. But he had made up his mind that no matter how much they yelled and screamed at him, he wasn't going to break down. They could go at him from now until sundown, and he wouldn't give them the satisfaction of seeing him cry. With an effort, he made his voice sound calm. "Tony and I were down in the laundry room, and Jay came in and said we had been talking. That's all."

"That's *all*. Two sweet little innocent kids down there in the laundry room, just making their clothes nice and clean and not saying a word to each other, right?"

"Right."

"Bullshit! You were talking to each other, and it looked like you were shaking hands!" It was Jay, whom he had come to consider a friend, saying this. And now this friend was leaning forward, elbows on his knees, glaring at him, challenging him. Adrenalin shot through David's system, and he longed to leap up and smash that squealing bastard—but he held himself down, arms folded tightly, and felt in control.

"Well, maybe just about how one of the machines wasn't working right or something like that."

Hoots of derisive laughter from the group. "You guys are on the ban, true? Because you knew each other on the outside, and you used to get high together, maybe do a little shoplifting together, stuff like that, right? And now you're going to tell us that when you're down in the basement doing your laundry together, like a couple of washerwomen, and nobody's around—or you *think* nobody's around—you're gonna talk about how the machine doesn't work?"

It sounded stupid even to David. But he didn't know what

33

to say. He sure couldn't tell them what they had actually been talking about. Everybody was watching him, waiting. Why him, why not Tony? Then they all started yelling, and he wondered how long he could stand it.

"Why you holding your belly like that?" Carla asked him.

He looked down, saw that his arms were wrapped tight across his stomach. "You got some guilt in that belly? You gonna cop to it *now*, Dave, or you gonna hang onto it for a while longer? 'Cause we all know you got it."

Suddenly he was very weary, very tired of the whole business. He felt as though they'd been pounding on him for hours. But what would Tony do if he told them what they were talking about in the basement?

And then he couldn't take it any longer. "We were saying whichever one of us could get hold of some grass first would bring some for the other one." He said it quietly, keeping his eyes on the patch on Tony's knee. Then he risked a glance at his face. Tony looked almost relieved.

"That all? That all you stupid creeps talked about down there? How about splitting? If you got a negative contract to get high, then I bet you got a negative contract to split, too. What else you got in that belly that's just bustin' to come out?"

"Nothing." That was the truth. He'd said it all, and somehow it felt better now that it was done. He couldn't have stood that pounding for much longer. But what was going to happen to him now? What would they do to him?

Kevin was working the ends of his mustache. "Okay, Dave, Tony, you two listen to this now: you're hooked up to the dishpan. You know what that means? It means you're out in the kitchen bustin' suds after every meal from now until I tell you different. You got that? And since you'll both be there, may I remind you gentlemen that you're *on the ban,* and if I hear about

34

a single word out of either one of you to the other, you're going to be in one hell of a lot more trouble. Is that clear?"

"Yes." Washing dishes, shit! And for how long?

He hated it. Some days he worked in the big sink, scrubbing an endless parade of stainless steel kettles and greasy baking pans. Other days he cleaned trays, scraped and rinsed dishes. The only thing that made it bearable was the general atmosphere in the kitchen, a bright, cheerful, busy place, and the friendly presence of Fred Kessler, the cook.

David liked being around food, and the meals at the Center were a lot better than the fungus they dished out at the high school. You could have a lot of it, seconds and even thirds if they didn't run out. The desserts were generally crummy though, mostly canned fruit. Someday, if he ever got out of this dishpan hookup, he thought he might like to work on the kitchen crew. Before he had come here he and Billy used to rip off a bunch of stuff at the supermarket once a week or so and cook up these really fantastic feasts. He could probably do something like that here.

But he was beginning to wonder if he'd ever get out of the dishpan. On the sixth day of his hookup he was hustling through some really mucky baking pans and the ramrod, the guy in charge of the kitchen crew, came over and told him the pans were still greasy and he'd have to do them over and do them right.

"Go screw yourself," David muttered, not loud but loud enough.

"And you quit reacting," the ramrod told him. "When somebody pulls you up for not doing the job right, you keep your mouth shut and you do it *right*."

Heat rose from his guts to his brain, and before he thought what he was doing was yelling, "Get off my back! Leave me alone! Go find somebody else to play big shot with!" And he knew as soon as the words were out of his mouth that he was in trouble again.

"What *is* it with you, Dave? What you got in your head instead of brains, man?" Not the big yellow-beard this time but Byron Hopkins, the tall black dude with flashy clothes and a dense Afro. "When you get hooked up, you do your job. When somebody pulls you up, you do not react. You just say yessir, and you keep on working. Only maybe this time you really bust your *ass*. And if you ever want to get off this hookup, brother, you better start learning now to control that big fuckin' *mouth* of yours. Because if you don't, you're going to spend more time in here getting killed than you are out on the floor learning something about yourself. You got that?"

Bending over the steaming dishwater, David counted up his time at the Center. Seven weeks, that's forty-nine days, and the last thirteen of them in a hookup. He had never believed he would last this long. Somtimes he hated it, like right now.

He was as low as you could get. Hookups—a nice way of saying fuck-ups, according to Kevin—were at the bottom of the pile. They'd done something wrong, and they were kept in some filthy job—if not dishes, then scrubbing bathrooms or walls or floors—until staff decided they'd learned something from it. You didn't even get a break to take a leak without staff permission.

Above the hookups were the service crews that did all the work around the place. He had been on the landscaping crew, mostly raking leaves, until he had gotten into this hookup. Sooner or later he'd probably get shifted around to housekeeping, or kitchen crew, or communications, which was all office work and sounded like the dullest.

Then after they had decided you were ready for some responsibility, they made you ramrod of the crew. And when you were really far along in the program, you got to be an expediter.

36

That was when you wore a necktie and good pants, not jeans, or a skirt if you were a girl, and you were on duty. And you ran errands for staff and kept an eye on things. Expediters watched everybody all the time, making sure nobody was breaking any rules, and if they caught you doing something wrong or even suspected you might be thinking something wrong, they pulled you up and then they ran and kissed staff's ass and reported whatever you were doing. And then before you phased out you could even get to be super ass-kisser, and get the job of shingle, a foreman over the other expediters.

For a moment, wiping his itching nose on his shirt sleeve, David imagined himself at the exalted level of expediter, notebook bulging in his hip pocket, carrying an important message to the staff office, pulling up some bastard who'd goofed off or was sneaking a cigarette. Forget it, he told himself. *I'll never make it to expediter. I won't stay.* . . .

Kevin Murphy eased his car out of Mrs. Bremen's narrow driveway and drove through a heavy October downpour the eight miles to the Center to start the afternoon shift. There was, as usual, no place to park since construction had begun on the new building. He found a place to wedge in along the shoulder of Old Ridge Road and walked down the steep driveway. Not much progress on the building; the idea was to have it under roof by the time the weather got bad, but the steady rains had slowed them down and they had only begun framing.

He had mixed feelings about this building program. The idea of expanding the Center didn't seem like a good one to him. When he had been in the program here seven years ago, it had been entirely different. Everybody had been much older for one thing; all in their late teens and early twenties, and most of them pretty heavily into heroin. In those days everybody was going for methadone, but it hadn't cured a thing. They said it was better than heroin, even though it was addictive, because you didn't need to keep taking more and more of it. It was cheap, too. You could stay high on it for practically nothing. But the high was never as good as it was when he was shooting smack.

Kevin sometimes wondered what would have become of him if he had not been dragged in here by his Uncle Barney. He hadn't been able to get along with his parents—his father was an alcoholic and his mother stayed spaced-out on tranquilizers—so he had moved in with his uncle in Brooklyn, a tough old bird, an ex-Marine sergeant. When Uncle Barney broke down the bathroom door and found Kevin out cold on the floor, he got him to the hospital and then gave him a choice: be locked up or go to a place out in the suburbs where a doctor he knew had started a program to help addicts. Kevin sweated for a few days and then came to the Center.

The doctor kept the place together by sheer determination, working with a dozen of them, guys like Kevin, feeling his way along, picking up some techniques from what he had read about drug treatment programs, adding his own innovations, knowing methadone wasn't the answer. It had been rough. Kevin had left once, started shooting again, come back. The second time he had made it. He was twenty years old when he came out, and he sometimes thought about all the wasted zero years before that. He wanted to go to college, but there wasn't any money and anyway he still didn't know what he wanted to do with his life. He was good with his hands, and he had gotten a job with a company making hand-crafted furniture. It paid fairly well and the work was all right. Then he signed up for a few night courses at the community college and tried to find out what he really wanted. Still he kept coming back to the Center, even after he graduated, just to keep in touch. Things were beginning to change there. It excited him.

After a year and a half he quit his job at the furniture company and took a job driving the van for the Center, even though he earned only about half as much. A few months later they signed him on as a counselor.

Now the kids who came to the Center were much younger. Fifteen or so seemed to be about average, with kids coming in as young as thirteen. The oldest were eighteen or nineteen. And heroin wasn't the problem any more. He couldn't remember when the last one came who used any heroin at all. Now they all were smoking grass, popping a rainbow of pills, sniffing whatever was breathable, anything for a high. And fighting with their parents, getting into trouble at school, having run-ins with the law. Incorrigible, they called them. Miserable was probably a better word.

The kids had changed, and so had the staff. It used to be that all the counselors were people who had been through the program, or one like it. There was absolutely nothing the kids could pull, nothing they could ever come up with, that we hadn't been through too, Kevin thought. They could run a line of shit past a professional, a social worker or even a psychiatrist, but never past us. We'd *been* there. A couple of years ago they had started adding people to the staff who didn't have their kind of practical experience, beginning with a psychiatrist and a social worker. Quite a few of the new counselors were people with college degrees.

Betsy was one of those. Lots of theory, not much experience. But he had to admit that Betsy was tuned into these kids. Probably just as tuned in as he was. Maybe they could run her some shit occasionally, but when it came right down to it, she knew how to handle them. And for the last couple of years, going to school at night, Kevin had been getting some of the theory, too. If he lived long enough he'd have a bachelor's degree in counseling.

Kevin thought most of the changes were good, but he hoped

they wouldn't add any more dormitory space; with more than a hundred kids it wouldn't be a family any more. It would be just another impersonal institution.

The director said the idea was to have most of the kids living there instead of letting half of them go back to their families each night. There was often something wrong in these families, one reason why so many kids were at the Center in the first place.

In Kevin's caseload, one boy had been beaten regularly by his father, a girl was raped by her mother's boyfriend, and at least two of the kids had parents who were alcoholic or borderline nuts. A couple of kids had never known their real fathers, and one boy was convinced he had not even *had* a mother. Fucked-up parents produced fucked-up kids.

Kevin thought about David Peterson. He had seen the parents a couple of times. Father seemed stiff, distant. Mother all smiles and nicey-nice but probably secretly hated the old man. David, in the middle, acted like a snot, but underneath all the crap there might lurk a decent kid. Seemed pretty bright, too. But a sneak, without a doubt; lied as easily as he spelled his name. Kevin wondered what was really eating the boy; wondered if David would stick with the program long enough to let them find out enough to help him. Kevin still had a tough time when a kid split. It had taken him almost three years to learn not to feel that he had somehow failed when that happened. The trick was to give everything you had as long as you were with the kids at the Center and then to forget about it as soon as you drove away.

In the second floor staff office Kevin fixed himself a cup of coffee and straddled the arm of the sofa, its upholstery worn through to the wooden frame. George Miller, the clinical director, with a string of initials after his name that stood for his various degrees in psychology, was already installed on the Barcalounger, and the rest of the staff had found places around the room. This was the second meeting of the day. The first had been at nine in the morning, and the next would be at four-thirty. Three times a day, except on weekends, the staff got together to catch up on situations that had arisen, kids who needed special attention, and practical problems like the imminent arrival of the fire inspectors, which sent everyone into a panic over violations created by tight space and tighter funds. Kevin was just beginning his shift; he'd be there until groups were over that night. He caught Betsy's eye; she had the wake-up shift, but she didn't look even faintly tired. He moved his gaze swiftly away.

George introduced a new person at the meeting, a spiffy type in expensive leather skirt and vest and a big diamond engagement ring. Pam Weis was studying for her master's degree in art therapy, and she'd be doing some experimental field work at the Center. She'd managed to talk a camera company into donating some instant cameras and film, and she was planning to organize some groups around this equipment. She wanted to meet with the OR staff to get some recommendations of kids who could benefit from her approach. Kevin thought David might be a good one for this.

"Anybody have anything to bring up?" George asked.

Plenty. Somebody shoved somebody else in the Greenhouse, and the second somebody shoved him back. Somebody else reacted when he was told to put out a cigarette. Somebody was rude to one of the teachers at the Center School. Somebody's VD test came back positive, which was a bit strange because the girl had been insisting she was a virgin. "Hanging out on the wrong toilet seats, no doubt," George suggested.

And somebody had split. Tom Plummer was at the Center school, and he went out to the boys' restroom and never came back. Kevin was relieved that it was not one of his kids, but Ted Valentine, Tom's primary counselor, reacted differently. "It's my favorite day of the week," he cracked, "when a sneaky creep like Tommy Plummer finally decides to improve my life and split. Have you ever tried talked to that kid? He sprays you with spit. It's like holding a conversation with a garden sprinkler. You have to wear a snorkle mask or drown before he gets to the end of a sentence." Creep or not, Ted had tried but failed to locate the boy's mother, and if he didn't show up by the end of the day they'd call his probation officer and notify the police.

They laughed at Ted's crack. The downbeat humor was one way to protect themselves from the emotional pressure. "You're sick!" George accused them. "You're all sick! You've been working here too long."

He might be right, Kevin thought. There were nights when he couldn't sleep; days when his stomach wrestled angrily with his food. They worked off some of the tension in staff meetings, making ghastly jokes about the kids, the kids' parents, themselves.

There had been a couple of attempts to regularize these staff meetings, rules laid down about obscene language and bad jokes about the kids. This was serious business, Dr. Stone said; young lives were at stake. And suppose some official from the state could hear this? Any outsider who happened to walk into a staff meeting would probably keel over. But efforts to sanitize the meetings had been a failure. It just didn't work, no matter what the rules were, and shutting off that one safety valve seemed not to be healthy.

Kevin wondered sometimes how all this sat with Betsy. It was a male domain, full of macho and ego and vulgarity. It always had been, except for Mrs. Cahill, the nursing director who had been at the Center since it first opened its doors and must have seen and heard everything by now but remained serenely unshakable and grandmotherly. When they started admitting girls to the program, they had to start putting women counselors on the staff. Kevin thought it must be rough for Betsy—the obscene language, the crude humor. She didn't flinch, but he had never heard her join in, either. Some day he'd have to ask her about it.

He reported that Peterson and Russo were still in the dish-pan.

"Have you seen the Peterson kid's parents lately?"

"I have to call them for another meeting this week."

"What are they like?"

"Your typical American couple. Mom's a marshmallow, Pop plays the heavy."

"Now, now. Be *nice*, Kevin. You, too, may be a parent some day."

The meeting broke off, and Kevin went to set up an after-noon encounter group. Then he had to find time to do his paper work, write up a couple of treatment plans, and talk to some of the new members. One of his top priorities was to spend some time alone with David Peterson. And he must not neglect to make that call to the parents. He was falling behind, wondered how he'd get everything done by the end of the semester. It looked as though it was never going to stop raining.

David stared at his chewed nails and waited for Kevin to ask him a question. He had mixed feelings about these sessions with Kevin. It was not like the groups, where somebody could con-front you, coming out of nowhere, it seemed, to rip into you. But in groups there was also the chance that it *wouldn't* happen, that you could slide through. Here in Kevin's office, though, you couldn't squirm away from his attention, his inquiring green eyes. David always found himself telling Kevin much more than he meant to. Sometimes he resented that, but sometimes it felt good.

"So how're you doing, Dave?"

"Pretty good."

"Things cool in the kitchen? Or you still coming off your belly when somebody tries to tell you something you don't want to hear?"

"It's cool."

"Yeah? Convince me."

David hesitated, holding back. Then he said, "There's this one kid. I feel like he's always squatting on me, just waiting for me to do something or say something, so he can make a pull-up."

"So what do you do about it?"

David shrugged. "Nothing. What can I do?"

"You know what you can do. Drop a slip on him. You dropped a slip on anybody yet? You write it down on a piece of paper, addressed to him from you, and you put it in the slip box down in the living room. Every couple of weeks we empty the box, and you'll be put in a group with him. Then you can confront him, tell him how you feel, and he'll probably come back and tell you how *he* feels."

Silence. "I don't know if I can do that."

"You got to learn. The one thing you're here for is to learn to handle your own feelings. After a while you'll be able to tell him right then you think he's squatting on you, without getting mad and blowing up. But you're not ready for that yet. You still lose your head too quick. So you drop a slip, and you take care of your feelings in the group. Try it. You'll learn a lot."

David nodded, licked his lips. He'd rather punch the son-of-a-bitch in the mouth.

"So what else is going on?" Kevin prodded him.

"Nothing."

"Come on, there must be something. How about you and that Tony Russo? You sticking to the ban?"

"Yeah, we don't talk." That was true. Hard, though.

"Why don't you tell me something about what you and Tony were doing on the outside. Was he your best friend?"

44

"No. We just got high together once in a while, and once or twice we ripped off some stuff from stores."

"Who was your best friend?"

David rubbed his hands on his jeans. "Billy Ehrlich. Him and me, we were really tight. More than anybody else."

Kevin seemed to be searching for something, looking for a warning signal. "How tight were you guys?" And he saw the flicker of fear in David's eyes.

"I don't know what you mean," David said dully, retreating.

"I think you do."

There was a long silence. Kevin let it go on. "You want to say anything?"

A single shake of the head. Then, almost in a sob: "I'm not a fag or anything like that. It just happened a couple of times." He was not like Nick, a boy with pale hair and paler eyes; David often took easy shots at Nick, sometimes mincing by him with a limp wrist when he thought Nick wasn't looking.

"How did it happen?" Gently, very quietly.

But David didn't want to talk about it or even think about the times in Billy's room, with the music on, the combination of pot and beer, of just wanting to be close to somebody. He had shoved it almost entirely out of his mind. *No!* He was going to forget about it; it hadn't happened.

But the next thing he knew he was crying, telling Kevin things he hardly even dared to let into his mind: things he had done with Billy. Misery and sweat and tears poured out of him.

Kevin handed him a tissue. "Do you think you're homosexual?"

"Yes. No. I don't know."

"Is that what you want to be?"

"No. But maybe I already am!"

"It's something you can change, you know. You have the choice. Just because you've had some homosexual experiences doesn't make you a faggot. Lots of people have gone through what you have. But they've changed. You can, too."

The talk ended soon after that. David, exhausted, stumbled down to the living room. Nick spotted him. "Hey, Dave, you want to talk?"

Terrified, David nearly fled from the room. But he didn't. The sweat cold on his body, he sat down at the opposite end of the sofa, according to the rules, and they started to talk. Somehow they got around to their fathers. They had something in common on that subject, certainly: both boys were afraid of the men. "I hate the son of a bitch," Nick said, speaking aloud what David had sometimes thought. But the feeling had always scared him, and he had never said it to anyone, not even to Billy, hardly even let it whisper in his own mind.

David couldn't quite decide how to pose in order to show the Real David. Whatever that was. He finally struck an aggressively macho pose with his arms gripped across his chest and a cigarette dangling from his lips. Felipe snapped his picture. When the print came out, he didn't like it, and they tried another. It didn't suit him either, but that was his last chance. While they sat around a table, Pam, the art therapist, led them through a yoga exercise of tensing and relaxing various parts of their bodies to get in the mood. Then she had them close their eyes, and she described a fantasy world to them: they were walking through a cool, dim, pine forest, then into a sunlit meadow, and finally through an opening into a secret place. "Imagine whatever you want, see whatever you want to see, do whatever you want to do, become whatever you want to become. Then become yourself again and come back here and draw that fantasy world."

While she talked, David followed her in his mind, slitting his eyes occasionally to see how other people in the class were taking it. One girl stared straight ahead, apparently afraid to close her eyes; another boy was also checking to see what the others were up to. When the journey ended, David cut out the photograph of himself, disliking the tough-guy pose that didn't fit the fantasy world he pictured. He eliminated all but the face, which he pasted on a large sheet of poster paper, making it the head of a huge mythical bird with a gigantic wingspread that flew high above a field of fire and over the massive wall that concealed the secret fantasy-place. David soared free and proud as a hawk riding the updraft, completely alone.

Pam asked them to talk about their pictures, but for some reason, David did not want to. She didn't pressure him, but the others in the class did. "What's the matter with *you*, Peterson? We've all talked about our pictures. What makes you so different?"

"I don't want to, that's all!" He wasn't quite sure why, but right now he didn't want to share anything with anybody.

"Davey's counselor called today," Ellen Peterson announced, passing the meat loaf and mashed potatoes.

"What's he say about Davey?" Susie wanted to know. She was surprised to find that she missed her brother. She used to think she couldn't stand him when he was tormenting her all the time. But now she wondered what was going to happen to him.

"He didn't really say anything. He wants us to come in and talk to him, Dick." Her husband nodded. "He suggested Thursday right after dinner. I said I'd ask you."

"Okay."

"I'm going to Parents Group tonight. Do you want to come?"

"Some other time."

He had been saying that for weeks, since the first time she mentioned it. "They have these meetings on Monday nights where you can talk about your family problems and so on.

47

Maybe we should go and see what it's about," she had said the week after David moved into the Center."

"I don't like clubs. You know that."

"It isn't a club. It's not social. It might help Davey."

Up to the last minute she had been undecided, hoping, but knowing better, that Richard would change his mind and go with her, that she would not have to walk alone into a strange group of people.

At her first meeting they gave her a name tag and a cup of coffee and tried to make her feel welcome. After the business meeting they sent her off with a group of other parents of new members of the program. Byron Hopkins was there from the Center to answer questions. At that moment she was glad Richard had not come with her. Richard was a very conservative man, and he had certain prejudices. He didn't care much for Negroes, which was the politest term he would use, and Byron was black. Richard didn't like beards, either, which was a problem because almost every male at the Center seemed to have one. Byron had a small goatee and a large Afro. She didn't object to the fact that Byron was black; she had worked with some nice black people at the hospital. She was sure they wouldn't hire somebody to work with the children who wasn't a nice person. Ellen had no idea that she, too, was prejudiced.

They met in a classroom at the Center School, pulling the seats into a circle. A good-looking man with prematurely gray hair and glasses addressed the small group of people, three couples and two other women alone, all nice, well-dressed people. Ellen was glad to see that she was not the only woman there by herself. The man explained that his son had graduated from the program a year ago and was doing fine and that he was there to tell parents of new members about how the Center was helping their children and how the Parents Group could help them.

48

Then they went around the circle and they all introduced themselves and told their stories, what their children were like, and how they had found the Center.

One of the women said she was divorced and told of how she had struggled with her daughter, who kept running away from home and getting involved with boys and so on. She often wondered if it would have turned out different if she had stayed married. She felt guilty, she said. Maybe none of this would have happened if she had not been divorced. She said that she had been lonely and unhappy, and maybe she hadn't paid enough attention to her daughter. Ellen glanced at the woman; she seemed close to tears and she had shredded a tissue into tiny wads.

They reassured her. Look at them, they said to her. They were all married and their kids had gotten into trouble, too. Ellen could feel the woman's loneliness and pain. I could never get a divorce, she thought. I could never go through the kind of thing this woman is going through. Richard and I might not have the perfect marriage, but what would I ever do if he left me? Suddenly she had been engulfed in panic, rising like nausea in her throat, a cold flush of fear.

"You go on without me," Richard was saying again, slicing the meat loaf. "Maybe I'll go some other time. Are there any more potatoes?"

"We have to save some for Richie."

She went alone again.

George Miller, dressed up in a windowpane plaid suit and Italian boots polished to a mirror shine, was there to give a talk about what he called "the profile child." Maybe they'd noticed the same thing—that their kids all seemed to have just about the same kinds of problems: the drugs, the trouble at school, trouble with the law, trouble at home. That was just the surface of things, he told them. Underneath that surface all kinds of things were going on. The kids hadn't learned to control their impulses. They still thought and acted like babies, because they felt like babies. Maybe they'd got some kind of learning problems that the schools hadn't picked up on. Maybe they had done okay in the lower grades, but when they got to junior high and high school they just didn't have what it takes, and their grades dropped and they started feeling bad about themselves.

Maybe there was something really wrong at home, too, George suggested. Sometimes one of the parents had emotional problems or drank too much; that was an easy one to spot. What was not so easy to see was when the family seemed to be getting along all right but really wasn't. Lots of times people didn't even know themselves that something was wrong. They thought everybody lived this way. But the *kid* knew. Probably not in his head, but down in his belly he sensed that something wasn't right. So he turned to his peers to get the kind of good feelings he wasn't getting at home. And those peers were more likely to be negative than positive influences, because they had problems at home, too. So the kid started cutting school, getting high, stealing, and so forth.

Ellen clutched her shoulders and listened. Was this what was going on in her family? Were they all really unhappy? Susie seemed to be doing all right, and so did Richie. If the two of them were okay, then what was the problem with David? She and Richard never argued any more. There were never any explosions like in some families she knew—not since the time a couple of years ago when he got mad at David and slapped her. But that was only once. It was true that she couldn't talk to him, but she hadn't been able to talk to her own father either.

The divorced woman raised her hand. "You've told us about

'the profile child,'" she said. "Is there such a thing as a 'profile family'?"

To answer her question, George Miller quoted the Russian novelist, Tolstoy: "All happy families resemble one another; every unhappy family is unhappy in its own way."

"I'd like to add something to that," the attractive man with gray hair said. "I've been around the Center and Parents Group for a few years now, and I've heard the same stories about kids over and over, but I don't think I've ever heard the same story twice about parents."

"One of these days," the psychologist explained, "we hope to have a family counseling program, to help the family get along well with the child. We're working on developing that right now."

Ellen did not want to face the specter of her own unhappy family. She felt guilty enough that one of her children was in so much trouble and needed help that she couldn't give him. What kind of mother was she, anyway? She had really worked hard at being a *good* mother. She had given up her nursing career and stayed home with the children the way Richard wanted her to. She had tried to do all the right things. She had even been involved in Cub Scouts when David was younger. But something had gone wrong, and she didn't know what. If it was her fault, she wanted to do something to change. Maybe somebody could tell her. Maybe she could raise her hand and say to George Miller, "Is it my fault?" But she wasn't sure she could stand it if he said yes. And what if he said, as he had just suggested, that there might be something wrong with the marriage? That couldn't be changed. Richard wouldn't let it.

When she went home, Richard was watching the late news on television. "How was it?"

"Fine. George Miller talked about the profile child. Very

interesting." She stood by his chair and waited until the sports and weather were over. "I want you to go with me next week," she said. "I believe it's important."

"I'll think about it," he said.

At least he hadn't said no. But she knew that's what he meant.

CHAPTER 3

"DAVID PETERSON! YOU'RE WANTED IN THE S.O.!"

His mind raced as he took the stairs two at a time to the second floor staff office, dreading to think what might be in store for him. Maybe another haircut. Not a physical haircut with an inch or two of hair chopped off, but a verbal haircut. He wondered where they ever found a term like that. Haircuts—the verbal kind—were pretty frequent. He hated them, standing there in the middle of the staff office, sometimes by himself, sometimes with whoever else had gotten into trouble—and getting killed, sometimes by Kevin or another counselor, usually with Paul Kendricks or one of the other high rollers around. They yelled at you, told you how stupid you were, what a jerk, what a jackass for whatever it was you'd done. Breaking one of the rules always got you some kind of a haircut, and there were dozens, maybe hundreds of rules. He had conquered the urge to scream back at them, had learned to stand and take it, to be told that he was hooked up again or had lost a privilege or whatever it was, without flinching, without reacting, without getting an attitude.

A couple of other guys from the service crew were already fidgeting in the S.O. Maybe that's what it was: the whole crew was getting a haircut.

"Okay, I'm going to make this short," Kevin said with mock ferocity. "You're all Intermediates, as of right now."

They all laughed with relief and pleasure and hugged Kevin and pounded each other on the back.

David had been at the Center for almost three months. He could hardly believe all the things that had happened to him. At first he had been determined not to stay; now he was just as determined to make it. Not every day; some days everything went wrong and he thought about leaving, and there were times when he would have given just about anything to get high again.

He worried about doing well. When he had asked Kevin a couple of weeks ago, Kevin had said, "You're doing okay, but I still think you're holding back a lot of stuff." Kevin had said David's complete about-face might have been part of the problem. "You're going around here acting like Mr. Positive, trying to be perfect. It's fine to want to do well, but I get the feeling in groups you don't want to look bad. You're afraid to talk about how you really feel, because then people might see that something is bothering you, and you wouldn't look so perfect after all. But the only way you're going to change is to let out some of those feelings, to talk about them, so you can learn to deal with them."

There was no end to the pressure on all of them. Even on weekends when the house was loose and he could sleep a little later and there were no groups, even then there was no letup. The crews still had to get their jobs done. After every meal and then again late in the evening, David's service crew folded up the chairs and tables in the dining room and swept and wet-mopped the floors, including the lobby. The vacuum cleaner had been broken for no one could remember how long, so the living room, carpet and all, had to be swept with a broom. The service crew ramrod, Doug Mitchell, had had David dusting, covering every inch of molding and shelf space, the tops of the picture frames, the little figures on the basketball trophies. Then he would come around and check, just like in the Navy or something. And when he finished there were still people who wanted to talk. Even when he sat down to play backgammon, it had to be with an older member, and they always got him into some kind of heavy discussion.

David was given a new job assignment as an Intermediate: kitchen crew. If anybody had told him a year ago he'd actually *enjoy* a job like this, he would have said they were nuts. But he liked it. It was hard work. The big pans of food were heavy, and it was easy to get burned. But it made him feel good that he could handle it, that he could cook things people liked to eat. Fred, the cook, planned the menus and bought the supplies, but the crew did all the actual cooking. David peeled potatoes, shredded cabbage for cole slaw, assembled the ham and cheese sandwiches that went into the oven, molded hamburger patties, mixed tuna fish salad. Sometimes, when somebody wanted to make something special, Fred showed them how. One of the girls got to be an expert on jellyrolls, and Fred promised David he'd teach him to make bread.

There was another change: David got a new primary counselor. Betsy Coleman.

Betsy had been reading David Peterson's file. She liked the boy, and when he made Intermediates she asked to have his case transferred from Kevin to her. Everything was in the file, neatly catalogued. First, the data sheet with names of parents, birth date and so on. Then the intake examination, done by Dr. Stone:

"White male, fifteen years of age, appears to be of average height and weight for his age. . . . At times seemed sullen and withdrawn but occasionally opened up and related fairly well. . . . No signs of psychosis, but does appear to have some hostile feelings toward his parents, particularly his father, and some incestuous feelings toward his mother. . . ." And so on. In the end, however, Dr. Stone concluded that David was appropriate for the program and would be admitted to the Center for the usual thirty-day period of observation and testing, beginning September 3. . . .

Betsy sighed. They always sounded so hopeless when they first came to the Center. She would seldom bet on any of them making it. She didn't believe she could take working in the Orientation part of the program with so many of the kids splitting during those first few months. You lost so many then that you almost hated to get involved enough to care, because every time one went it could really hurt. But you couldn't *not* get involved either, because it was the involvement, the caring, that kept them here. They didn't come in with any motivation; in fact, most of them were here against their will. It was the friends they made with staff and with other kids that meant the difference between staying and making it or splitting and going back to their old lives.

There were, of course, a lot of splittees in the Intermediate phase, too. Many of them came back and endured whatever they had to go through to be allowed to stay. Some never came back. But some returned and left again. What was really heartbreaking was when a kid went all the way to Phase-Out, almost to graduation, and then split.

Betsy flipped through David's file. All the treatment plans had been filled out in Kevin's neat handwriting: the problem, the objective, the way he intended to approach it, target dates for solving it. A lot of it seemed to be working. For instance, poor group participation, difficulty in expressing feelings, and few peer relationships that were the main problems in David's early days at the Center seemed to be improving. Betsy had watched him in a few groups and agreed with Kevin's observations that David was getting better at confronting people. An ace, in fact, at seeing other people's problems, but he still had trouble perceiving where he ought to make some changes himself.

There was still a lot of acting out; his mouth often got him into trouble, but at least it wasn't his fists. The reports from school were fairly good. Each time Kevin saw David, either in individual counseling sessions or in a group, he had filed a brief report—and so had everybody else who saw David. They showed the standard two steps forward, one back, and sometimes two or three back.

"A good kid," Kevin had written. Betsy agreed, but sometimes the good kids fooled you. They were so busy trying to protect their nice-guy images that they weren't willing to take any risks, to let themselves open up—privately to counselors, publicly in groups or even on the floor with their friends. So many of the problems that had gotten them into trouble in the first place were kept concealed and festering. Betsy wondered if she'd be able to probe into David's hidden places. Kevin had done his job well: he had gotten David involved and helped him through those first rough weeks of being away from home, of trying to express his feelings, of learning something about honesty, of making those first important friendships that would keep him committed to the Center and would eventually help to make him a whole and relatively happy person.

Now it was Betsy's job to pick it up and take it from there. Most of the fundamental changes that any boy or girl went through at the Center happened at the Intermediate stage. David would have to begin to develop some insight into whatever his real problems were. It wasn't enough that he hadn't gotten high or stolen anything for several months. Now he had to find out what was going on in his head that made it so important for him to steal and get high in the first place, to hang out with the wrong kinds of friends, to get into so much trouble with his parents, to perform so dismally at school. He would have to junk the old values that had gotten him into such a mess. And he'd have to adopt new values and really believe in them down in his gut.

Honesty, for instance. Complete honesty, not just an honesty of convenience. Nothing, not the slightest deviation from total honesty, was too small or insignificant to ignore. When these values were really woven into his beliefs, and his behavior was controlled by what he believed rather than by somebody else's rules and regulations, the Intermediate phase would be over, and the process of getting him reinvolved in the outside world would begin. Then Betsy would pass him along to a Phase-Out counselor. If he lasted that long. There was so much that could happen in the next year or so, between now and graduation.

Betsy Coleman loved her job, but it wasn't what she had planned to do with her life. When Betsy graduated from a private girls' prep school and announced that she wanted to be an actress, her wealthy, indulgent father had sent her off to an exclusive college with a theater department. She also had taken a number of courses in psychology, because it interested her. Degree in theater arts in hand, she had gone to New York and tried to get a job as an actress, sharing an apartment with three other girls on the Upper West Side. One of them would get a job as a secretary with a temporary agency to pay the rent while the others went out on casting calls. She had found that she hated that side of the theater. She wasn't even sure she liked New York, although she had gone there with a heart full of enthusiasm.

She also had had an unhappy love affair, an engagement abruptly broken off a few weeks before the wedding. On a recuperative weekend visit to her widowed father in the suburbs, a friend told her about someone he knew who was working at the Center. Betsy stopped by, just to see what it was like. There were no job openings, but they needed a volunteer to organize some outside programs for the kids. It paid nothing, and in order to do it she had to live at home again and borrow money from her father. She disliked that, but New York had gone sour and she was ready for a change. She told herself it was temporary and took the position. Two months later when a job opened up for a counselor, they hired Betsy. She had been there for almost a year now.

There was something about being around the Center kids that affected her. It hadn't taken her long to get close to them and for them to get close to her. Within a few months she had a full caseload. She rarely thought of her dreams of being an actress, and she didn't miss living in New York at all. She was even beginning to get over the man with whom she had once been in love. She rented a bright, airy room in a huge house from a woman painter. Life began to get better. She was considering studying for a master's degree in social work, although the idea of going back to school again was distasteful. Work at the Center was demanding, and the schedule of hours fluctuated constantly. At first she had put in a lot of extra time, but that had left her none for herself. She needed to unwind, so she went back to her old hobby, photography, and on her days off she roamed around shooting pictures. The woman from whom she rented the room allowed her to set up a darkroom in the basement.

When her shift was finished, Betsy replaced David's case history in the file drawer and walked through the muddy parking lot. Minutes later she had managed to get her small car stuck in a slippery rut. She tried putting gravel under the wheels, but the car dug deeper, and her clothes were wet and muddy.

Then she saw Kevin watching her struggle, a big grin on his face. As a feminist, Betsy did her best to take care of herself, as she had once told Kevin. He let her struggle just long enough to make his point.

"I'd help anybody in this situation, Betsy," he said putting his shoulder against the car and shoving. "Even Paul Kendricks." Paul was big enough and strong enough to lift a car like Betsy's out of the mud with his two large hands. Betsy watched Kevin in her rearview mirror, grateful for the help. She was glad to be alone with him for a few minutes, even with mud on her face. She wanted to invite him to come to her place for some hot chocolate, to hear some records, maybe even to look at some of her photographs. But she didn't, and he didn't say anything either.

"How'd you like to go home next Saturday—for the whole weekend?" Betsy asked David.

David had been waiting for this. It wasn't his first visit home; a couple of times before he had spent the day there, coming back to the Center at night.

The first time had been awful. His mother had picked him up Saturday morning. In the three months before that, he had talked to her on the phone a few times and had sat with her and his father in the office when they came in to meet with Kevin. But this was different. He had taken Jay along for strength—moral support for that first anxious visit. He had introduced Jay and they had climbed in the back seat, since Susie was occupying the front. David thought his mother looked different in some way; maybe she was doing something new with her hair. Susie looked different too; not like a little girl any more. Funny what a few months could do. He wondered if he looked different to them.

As soon as they reached the house, David rushed up the stairs to his room. He was ashamed to think of the mess he had left. Probably his mother had cleaned it all up herself. He wouldn't be like that now. At the Center you had to make your bed and keep everything straightened up all the time. For a while his roommate, Eddie, had pulled him up almost every day about his sloppiness. Now he kept things in order, but he wasn't sure he'd do it if there weren't somebody there to check on him. His mother always had said she had better things to do than to nag him all the time about his room. If he chose to live in a pigsty, that was his business. His father had wanted to fine him every day he didn't make his bed or hang up his clothes. But that, like most of the other systems of discipline his parents tried to impose, had been a failure. Nobody had had the time or the energy at home to monitor him and his actions twenty-four hours a day. At the Center, that's all they had to do. It was almost impossible to get away with anything.

On that first visit home after three months, he had flung open the door to his room and stopped cold. The orange walls had been painted bright blue, there were new curtains, the furniture was all different. He recognized the fancy canopy bed; Susie's stuffed animal collection occupied the shelf space under the windows. Stunned, David had backed out of his old room and stumbled down the hall to the little room that used to be Susie's. All of his gear had been crammed into the smallest of the three bedrooms, and although the ruffly curtains had been taken down, the walls were still pink. Pink! Nobody had asked him about changing rooms. He felt as though he had been drummed out of the family.

Downstairs his mother had poured some milk and set out a plate of his favorite nutless brownies. There were deep frown lines between her eyes. "You didn't give me a chance to tell you," she had said. "Susie moved into your room about a month ago.

She really needs it because of all the storage space. We just left the colors the way they were, so you can decide how you want to fix up the other room when you come back home."

"It doesn't matter," he had said. But it did. How could they have *done* this?

And this time he was actually going to have to sleep in that shitty pink room.

Betsy had told him to choose an older member of the Center to go along with him. This time he had decided to invite Doug, a broad-shouldered boy who chewed gum incessantly. Douglas made Intermediates about the time David came to the Center, and lately they had started to get tight. They had put in their request for the weekend visit at the Wednesday night meeting, when everybody who wanted to do something on the weekend had to get approval of their plans—to go to a Friday night movie, to go shopping Saturday afternoon, to go home. Many Intermediates, who had been in the program a long time and were nearing the time to phase out, went home regularly on weekends. Most of them seemed glad about it, but some had to be pushed. Annie Powell, for instance, would stay at the Center forever if staff would let her. But sooner or later she had to go home to live with her family again until she was old enough to be out on her own, and staff insisted that she must start getting used to it.

David tried to think about all the good things connected with going home. His mother would cook all his favorite dishes for him. Susie would be glad to see him. Maybe Richie, too. His brother was okay, he guessed; the two of them hadn't been tight for a long time, and David didn't really know what Richie thought about any more or how he felt. What he was really worried about was how it was going to go with his father. Before, on the one-day visits, everybody had watched television most of the time, and that had solved the problem. With more time, they were bound to talk. He was afraid of that. As Betsy told him, that was the reason for taking someone along from the Center—not just to keep him company, but to bolster him up in case things got rough.

"Don't worry so much about it ahead of time, Dave," Betsy advised. "Maybe it will work out just fine. And if it doesn't, maybe you'll find out some things you have to work on in groups."

David made introductions and he and Doug tossed their duffle bags in the rear of the station wagon and climbed in the back seat again. His mother seemed nervous, too. She had trouble getting the wagon turned around in the driveway. "Look out!" Susie screeched. "You almost hit that parked car."

Off to a good start, David thought. "What's new, Susie?"

"I made the school chorus."

"Hey, that's neat."

"But Daddy won't let me go with them on the tour this spring. He says I'm too young," she complained.

"The tour is still a few months away," her mother said. "Maybe he'll change his mind."

"Daddy's *mean*." Susie pouted. "I never get to do anything."

Oh-oh, David thought. "Where *is* Daddy?"

"He had to go into the office for a few hours this morning. He'll be back around noon."

"I'll show you around," he said to Doug when they arrived at the house. Not the bedroom yet, but the outside of the house. The early December wind made their eyes water, but they decided to walk up to Gemberling's Variety Store to pick up some cigarettes. If Mrs. Gemberling would let him in. He used to rip off stuff from the old lady, and he figured she knew it. There would be no browsing around. Just buy the cigarettes and leave. But Doug remembered that he needed a toothbrush and went to the back of the store to find one. David leafed through the magazines at the rack by the door under Mrs. Gemberling's un-

62

friendly stare. At that moment Billy Ehrlich came in, blowing on his reddened hands.

Billy spotted him and grinned. "Hey, man! I thought they had you locked up for good at that place."

David swallowed hard. "No, nothing like that. I'm home for the weekend with my friend Doug." He nodded toward Doug, who was still deciding among firm, medium, and soft bristles.

"Can you get away from that dude?" Billy asked. "I got some terrific stuff. My brother brought it back from Mexico."

David shook his head and stuffed his hands in his pockets to keep them from trembling. "Can't. No way can I do it. Besides, I don't get high any more."

Billy started to let out a bleat of laughter and then clapped his hand over his mouth. "Don't give me that bunch of shit! When was the last time you got high?"

"The night before I went there. When I was with you."

"Nothing since then? Man, you must be really strung out! I couldn't imagine you going three months like that!" He moved closer to David. "Hey, don't you miss it? Used to make you feel so good, right?"

Panicking: was it pot he was talking about? Or something else? He wished Doug would find a toothbrush and come back. But he couldn't quite break away from Billy.

"Listen, Dave, I'll wait for you on my bike between midnight and one. You watch for me. And then we'll go party."

"I can't, Billy. I honest-to-God can't."

"Look, I'll be there. You come out, it's fine. You don't, it's fine too. We used to be friends, but if you got something else going for you, then forget it."

"We're still friends, but I just can't. Listen, they moved my room. I'm in the back now, where Susie used to be."

They noticed Doug coming down the narrow aisle, and

Billy started to drift away toward the door. "Good seein' you, Dave. Take it easy." And he was out the door before Doug reached them.

"Who was that, Dave?"

"An old friend."

"Negative?"

"Yeah."

"You used to get high with him?"

"Yeah."

"So what were you talking to him about?"

"Nothing. Just telling him about the Center, and so on, and he was telling me about some of the other guys." He was lying, but he just couldn't tell Doug the truth. He knew he could be in deep trouble for saying even that much to Billy. And there was still some weird kind of bond with him, a desire to go with him and get high again. He saw Doug studying him as though he knew, and he turned away. "Let's go back home."

Richie had just gotten up and, still bleary-eyed, was stumbling around in the kitchen mixing himself a breakfast of raw eggs, bananas, milk, and ice cream, whirled in the blender. He shook hands with David and Doug when they came in, stomping from the cold, and poured out glasses of his concoction for each of them.

David felt shy around Richie for some reason, and he was glad again that Doug was there with him to take the edge off. Dave and Doug sipped their drinks, but Richie downed his in a hurry and chased it with a tall glass of orange juice.

"So tell me what it's like over there at the Center. You decided to stay?"

David watched his brother guzzle the orange juice and caught a glimpse of his pinkish eyes. He glanced at Doug and knew he had noticed it, too. So Richie got high now; what else was he into? David wondered if his parents knew. Perfect

Richard Junior, father's favorite, the next head of the family, wasn't so perfect after all. In a way it made him feel better, that he wasn't the only fuck-up in the family. But it bothered him, too. It would be just Richie's luck to be able to handle it without getting caught—to get high and party all the time and enjoy himself and still get good grades and do all the things his father expected. David had always been the one who got caught, even when they were little kids, playing together. If a window got broken or something was lost, it was always David who got the blame. Never could get away with anything.

"Yeah, I'm going to stay, I guess. It's a pretty good place."

"I can't imagine you putting up with all those rules, Davey. You never were good about rules."

"I can't imagine it either. But I do."

"There's a guy in my biology class at school, Marty Crowell? He split from the Center about six months ago, he told me. He says he just couldn't take it any longer. Every time he turned around, they were on his back about something. He said he figured he could get along without that crap."

"Marty and I used to be real close friends at the Center," Doug said. "He was one of the first people to pull me in. But he just couldn't get over the idea that he wanted to get high all the time. Finally he split. I wondered how he was doing. How *is* he doing?"

"Fine, I guess. He's stoned most of the time."

"Then he's not fine." Doug looked as though he felt like crying.

"He told me he was going to split," Doug told David later. "And I tried to talk him out of it. Once or twice I got him to stay. We were roommates. But one day I guess he just made up his mind and left without telling me. It really hurt. And then a couple of times I saw him around town, but I wasn't allowed to talk to him. I had to pretend he didn't even exist."

65

David didn't hear the car come into the driveway. He and Doug were playing chess, trying to concentrate against the chatter of the television show Susie was watching and the blare of Richie's rock music upstairs.

"Welcome home, stranger." His father was busy threading his woolen scarf through the sleeve of his coat and hanging the coat in the hall closet. Startled, David stood up suddenly, knocking over some of the chess pieces.

"Hi, Dad." They faced each other awkwardly. "Dad, this is my friend, Doug."

His father went over to shake Doug's hand, but he didn't touch David.

While they were trying to figure out what to do next, his mother called them for lunch. She had made liver dumpling soup and put out a big plate of cold cuts, and there was a giant bottle of Pepsi and more brownies. David hadn't had a chance to get hungry again, but he couldn't disappoint his mother. She had even set the table in the dining room, as though it was a special holiday. She fussed over them, serving them, keeping the conversation going with bright questions. Richie had become very quiet, and Susie looked bored. David wondered what was going on in her mind. His father said nothing.

It was good to be home in a way, but in another way it was not like being *home* at all, not like it was before. Nobody acted quite the same. His mother was trying too hard, practically suffocating him with attention and food. His father remained distant; only now he seemed light years away instead of only a million miles.

"Well, how's it going, Davey?"

"Good. Real good, Dad."

"You staying out of trouble?"

"Oh yes." That was really all he cared about: whether

David was *behaving*. David wished he could say to his father, "Look, I'm somebody different now. I'm changing. I'm not as bad as I used to be." He hoped his father saw that, but he was pretty sure he didn't.

Then David noticed his mother noticing Doug's table manners. She had been drumming on him since he was a little kid: sit up straight, keep your elbows off the table, don't slurp your soup, use your napkin. Not that he put much stock in all of this, and he certainly never thought about it at the Center, but at his mother's dining room table, which even had a cloth on it and the good china as though it was Christmas or Easter, he found himself sitting up straight, being careful not to slurp, and observing Doug, who leaned over his bowl full of soup and crumbled crackers and gripped his soup spoon as though he were shoveling cement. David saw his mother watching all of this, although she said nothing—she would never say anything to somebody else. David felt his face grow hot, first with embarrassment and then with anger. Doug was a great guy; what difference did it make if he didn't know all the rules of etiquette? His mother was judging his friend on the wrong basis.

Somehow David could not relax. He jumped every time the phone rang, which was constantly, but it was always for Susie. She seemed to live on the telephone. But late in the afternoon, while they were all watching television in the family room, there was a call for David. He was half-afraid to answer, and he knew Doug was watching him.

It was not Billy this time but T.J., another one of the old gang. "Hey, man, welcome home! You gonna stay here now?"

David muffled his end of the conversation. No, just home on a visit. No, the place was okay. No thanks. No, really. He didn't get high any more. No, no he couldn't come out. He hung up, catching Doug's eye.

Doug steered him back to the kitchen. "That the same guy you ran into this morning?" David shook his head. "He want you to come out and get high?"

"Yeah. But I told him no." However, David still did not tell Doug about the conversation with Billy that morning at Gemberlings.

Dinner was another huge meal. His mother had roasted a chicken and made mashed potatoes, his favorites. There were vegetables and a salad, too, but she didn't try to make him eat any, the way she used to. Susie had even baked a cherry pie especially for him and served him a huge piece loaded with vanilla ice cream. He wasn't sure he could finish it all, but he didn't want to hurt anybody's feelings. His stomach was tight, and he wished he and Doug could carry their dishes out to the kitchen and go right back to the Center. But there was tonight to get through, and then tomorrow.

They returned to looking at television. His father watched him light a cigarette. "I see you're still smoking. How many packs a day?" Richard had quit smoking a few years ago, and it was one of the things his father liked to harp on now.

"Just one."

"That's one too many. I'm surprised they let you smoke at the Center."

He and Doug tried to explain that almost everybody did and the staff discouraged it, but every time they tried to ban smoking, so many kids got caught sneaking cigarettes that they gave up and tried to work out something else. "We're under a lot of pressure as it is," David told his father. "I guess they figure it's not the worst thing we could be doing."

Richard Peterson did not agree. First of all, he lectured, he couldn't see that they were under any kind of pressure. What did they do all day? Just sit around and *talk?* Kids like them should be out working their butts off; maybe they'd learn something that way. Best thing, hard physical labor. He admitted he didn't really know anything about this modern psychology business, but it seemed to him that kids today were spoiled, that was the whole trouble. They didn't have any respect for their families, for their teachers, for anything or anybody.

"Guess you saw there've been some changes upstairs since you left."

"I saw that when I was here before," David said. Maybe his father was going to apologize.

"Your mother and I figured those who are here should be able to have what they want. And as soon as you've shown that you deserve it, we'll give you permission to fix up that back bedroom to suit yourself."

Anger winding up inside him like a spring, David wondered what would prove to his father that he deserved a nice room *now*. He was changing; he had been through a million changes already. But his father still saw him as just the way he used to be.

"You should be helping your mother with the dinner dishes," he added.

Why me, David wondered. Susie disappeared up to her room as soon as they had finished, and Richie went out immediately, hardly able to sit through dessert. David felt guilty. His father had always been an ace at making him feel guilty. But his mother shooed him away when he went to the kitchen with a belated offer of help. "I just want you to relax and *enjoy* yourself," she said.

David was glad when it was finally time to go to bed. He didn't even have the energy to stay up for the late movie.

His mother wanted to fix up the fold-out sofa for Doug in the family room, but Doug said he'd just as soon put his sleeping bag on the floor in David's room. They didn't talk much. There was a lot to say but also a lot of time to say it in later. Unable to fall asleep, David listened to Doug's steady breathing.

Sometime after midnight he saw the flashlight shine on his ceiling. Billy's code: two shorts, two longs. He crept out of bed, slid open the window, and leaned out. "Yo, Billy!" he called softly.

"You coming?"

"I can't."

"You chicken or what?"

"I'm not chicken." Doug turned restlessly on the floor, and David waited until he settled down again. "I'll be down in a couple of seconds. Just to talk, for five minutes."

He pulled his jeans on over his pajamas, found his down jacket, and, before he left, remembered to stuff some clothes and pillows in his bed in case Doug woke up. He slipped out through the garage to where Billy was waiting on his motorcycle. "Look, Billy, I just can't go with you."

"What can they do to you?"

"Nothing and everything." He was beginning to be sorry he had come this far. "Billy, I want to make it there."

"We can't talk here. Come on. I'll just take you over to my place. You can tell me about it. There's nothing wrong with talking, is there?"

"Yes, because you're a negative person. I can't do it."

Billy looked angry, sullen. "You mean after all the stuff there was between us, we can't be friends any more? What kind of bullshit place is it, anyway? You got balls or not?"

"Okay, but just for an hour. If Doug wakes up and finds out I'm gone, it's all over for me."

Was it an hour? Two hours? More than that? He couldn't remember later. He didn't get high, because he knew Doug would spot it right away. But he drank a can of beer, and then a second one. There were other guys there, and to keep from looking like a fool in front of them, he agreed with them that the Center was a bunch of faggots, people without the balls to make it on their own. After a while he persuaded Billy to take him home again. At least he hadn't gotten high, and Doug still seemed to be sound asleep.

The endless weekend finally ended. David's father took them back to the Center. For once there seemed to be a flicker of warmth in the old man's eye; or did he imagine it, because he wanted to see it there?

"I think you're on the right track, Davey," he said. "Keep it up." And he drove away.

"So how was your weekend, Dave?" Betsy asked. There was something about the look in David's blue eyes that bothered her. She didn't trust him. "Everything go okay at home?"

"I guess so. I was pretty nervous, but so was everybody else. My brother Richie gets high now. I don't know if he used to or not. And I guess it won't be long now until my little sister does, too. I think she runs around with her friends too much, but my parents let her get away with murder. And I know they don't know about Richie."

"Yes, but how about you? How did you get along with them?"

"Mom was nervous and kept feeding us, whether we were hungry or not, and we kept eating to make her happy. My dad was okay, just the way he usually is. Gave me a big lecture on why I ought to quit smoking. He thinks we're pampered here. Ought to be out digging ditches or something. And not smoking. But he seemed pretty good, I guess."

"So what else happened? Any of your negative friends try to make contact?"

David answered carefully, choosing his words. "I saw Billy —you know the one?—in the store, and we just said hi. And I guess he told T.J. I was home, because he called and wanted me to come out with him. And I said no."

"And that's all? You didn't see anybody else, didn't talk to anybody else?"

The palms of his hands were clammy. "No, that was it."

On the way down from the office, he saw the big sign above the front desk: HONESTY. And he thought he was going to be sick.

From then on things started to go wrong. A couple of days later, a heavy girl with bad skin accused him in a feelings group of calling her an ugly bitch and demanded tearfully why he had done it. Miserable, he admitted that he had. "Why?" they shouted at him, "You got some bad feelings you got to get rid of? Why you takin' it out on Carole?"

He didn't know; an easy shot, maybe. She got on his nerves somehow.

Somebody remarked that something was different with him lately. Others agreed. So what was up? "You got some guilt?" one of them demanded. "You been gettin' high or something?"

"I don't have any guilt," he said, looking the accuser straight in the eye.

"Bullshit!" the boy yelled at him. "Something's sure been bothering you. You been coming off to everybody lately. And I bet it's guilt."

For an hour they pounded him, yelling, shouting, accusing. "Why you holding your belly like that? Why you got your arms folded like that? You so full of guilt you can hardly sit up straight. You're like Noah, carrying a whole *boat*load of guilt, probably two of everything! So why don't you let it out? You been here long enough to know you'll feel better when you cop."

"Because I don't have any guilt!" he roared back at them, the very guilt they were talking about cramping his stomach.

"Don't you come off like that!" they warned him. "Don't you go getting an attitude around here! When somebody asks

72

you a question, when somebody confronts you, Peterson, you *answer!*"

"I don't have any guilt," he repeated, quietly this time. His head was roaring. All he could hear was the rising clamor of their voices. The pressure inside him seemed too much to bear. What if he told them what had happened, about going out to meet Billy and drinking those two cans of beer? A haircut. A general meeting, an apology to the Center family. Lose his job position. Get hooked up again for God knows how long. Back to the bottom, losing all his privileges, all his standing, just because of one stupid thing. Maybe even get put back into OR. There were people in the group who had been at the Center no longer than he had, and they were doing a lot better than he was. He could see that. He envied them. Maybe that was the reason he came off to Carole, calling her an ugly bitch. Besides, she wasn't really so ugly. Actually she was a nice person. He knew he was jealous of her. Calling her an ugly bitch made him feel—what? A little superior? Not really. He didn't quite know what was happening to him, but he felt like a shit. Maybe they were right—it was the guilt that was doing it. Maybe he should cop to it now, get it over with, take whatever he had to take. Kevin had told him once, and he had heard it from older members, "If you've got guilt, you either cop to it eventually or you split. But you just can't live with it in your belly. Your belly will flip every time somebody talks about guilt, or somebody does something like what you've done. It doesn't matter how small or how big. You never forget about it, even if you think you have."

Eventually they gave up on him and got off his case. The relief was immense, but it didn't last long. He made it through one group, but the next group got on him again. They knew he had guilt, sensed it somehow, and they weren't going to let him alone until he copped to it. He was in misery. He didn't think he could face the consequences, but he didn't know how much longer he could hold out in the face of all this pressure. So he was tense, nervous, restless and snotty. It seemed to him that everybody was watching him, just waiting for him to do something wrong. And he seemed to do everything wrong, almost as though he had to live up to their expectations.

He began to think about leaving. Any place would be better than this. Walking up the driveway at night to the Greenhouse, he looked at the narrow, tree-lined path that led away from the main house to the street. They called it the Splittee Path, and he pictured himself running under those trees, away from there. He didn't know just when it would be, or how, but he knew he was not able to take it much longer.

And then, the next time they were alone together, Betsy hit him with something else.

"How many good friends have you got here in the program? Is there anybody here you love?"

David had been struggling with this. It was one of the ideas that had struck him as just plain ridiculous the first time he heard about it: that you could get really close, really tight enough with somebody in the program to say, "I love you." He couldn't remember ever talking about this kind of stuff at home. Certainly his father had never said he loved him. He wondered if his father ever had said it to Richie or Susie. Probably Susie; almost certainly Susie. Maybe Richie. But not him.

Sometimes he had wished he could tell his mother he loved her, but it seemed such an embarrassing thing to say. Once in a while she used to come up and give him a hug and say, "I love you, Davey," but he had always pulled away from her and she stopped doing it.

"This is your family now, Dave," Betsy said to him. "It really *is* a family, and when you can get really close to somebody and you're willing to take some responsibility for that relationship, then you're ready to tell that person you love him. Girls, too. It's okay to love girls, as long as you do it in the right way. You have a sister, don't you?"

"Yeah. Susie."

"Do you love her?"

"I guess so."

"So just imagine if she were really close to you, your best friend. Could you tell her you love her?"

"I don't know."

There was somebody, though. Jay, the kid who first took him around, the one who went with him that first visit home. There was something about Jay that David really liked, and he and Jay had a lot in common. They both liked the same kind of music, and even the same rock groups. Jay had told Dave that for a while when he first came to the Center and even after he had made Intermediates, he used to put on his favorite albums, and the first thing he knew he was off on a trip again, thinking about getting high, missing his old friends. It often had made him feel like leaving. Finally he had mentioned it in a group, and the kids were all over him.

"Don't listen to the music, if it makes you feel that way!" somebody had yelled at him. He knew they were right. And he was put on the ban for music. It had nearly killed him. Jay had thought he couldn't survive without it. But somehow he had known they were right. After a while he got used to it, and then finally he didn't think much about it any more. He could listen now, but the crisis was over and he no longer felt his whole life depended on listening to his tapes.

Jay had once told David about the time he had split and how hard it had been to come back and face the family again. But he knew when he was out there, even while he was rolling the joints and laughing and joking with his old friends, that he wouldn't be able to make it without the Center. He had realized that his old friends only helped him get into trouble; that was all they ever did for him. During David's early days at the Center, Jay kept telling him "Your real friends are here, not out there. When you understand that, you'll stop thinking about leaving all the time, and you'll start trying to change."

Jay was right. Pushing the memory of his hours with Billy and the lies that had followed into a small black knot at the bottom of his mind, David made a decision. "Hey," he told Betsy, "I think I want to tell Jay I love him."

"Sounds good," Betsy said.

An hour later David found Jay on the stairway outside the kitchen and told him, and the two boys hugged each other and slapped each other on the back and David felt almost right again.

But then a peculiar thing happened. Suddenly, it seemed, Jay was doing things that irritated David, and a few days later when Jay pulled him up for something stupid, like leaving his jacket in the living room, David reacted. "Go screw yourself, Jay! Sometimes I get the feeling you're watching me, just waiting for me to do something wrong."

"Drop a slip, if you feel that way, but you better not come off to me like that again."

David stuffed a note into the slip box, and the next week they were put into a group together. David's mouth was dry when he asked to change seats with one of the girls so he could sit opposite Jay. He hoped he'd be able to talk; his voice felt hoarse and shaky. But then he plunged into a confrontation. "Jay, I want to know why you're squatting on me all the time. It feels like every time I turn around, you're there just waiting for me to do something wrong. So I want to know what's up with you?"

David was all anger and frustration, but Jay's reply was calm and reasonable. I'm not squatting on you. But I think you got a lot to learn around here. Your attitude is just generally lousy. You're sloppy, you just kind of drag around, you don't seem like you're going any place. And when somebody pulls you up about something, you really come off. You got a jacket for that—a reputation for coming off real mad. I think the question is more like, what's up with *you?*"

Furious, David shouted at him. "I'm trying to do good around here! But it seems like nothing ever suits you. I mean, you act like you're my goddam *father* or something!"

"Is that how your father treats you, Dave?" Betsy cut in.

Startled, David turned to her. "Yeah! Nothing I ever did was right. No matter how hard I tried, nothing ever pleased him. And he was always at me, telling me how to do things, telling me I'm not as smart as my older brother, Richie, telling me Richie would have done it the right way."

"So how does that make you *feel*, Dave?" one of the girls asked.

"It makes me feel like shit."

"Why don't you talk about that, Dave? Talk about how you feel about your father."

But he couldn't. It had taken only gentle pressure to get him to open up this much. Then he thought about the guilt, and he was afraid he'd let that go too, so he pulled back.

"There's more, isn't there, Dave?"

He shook his head.

"Listen, my dear," Betsy was saying, "Jay hasn't been squatting on you. One of your problems—at school, at home—is that you get mad and come off any time somebody criticizes you. Your father, schoolteachers, cops, anybody."

David glanced sheepishly at Jay. Him too. He knew Jay really loved him.

"And another thing. If you love a person and care about him, you tend to take pull-ups more seriously, to let them mean

77

something they don't. The closer you let yourself get to people, the more risk there is of getting hurt. You'll see that, but that doesn't mean you avoid the closeness. It's something that happens to everybody, all through life."

David listened and nodded, and the stone of his unconfessed guilt grew heavier.

Things were not going well for Kevin Murphy either. He was falling behind with his course work at the university. His car broke down and repairs put a large dent in his small savings. He sometimes thought he should quit this job and find one that paid a decent salary. The problem was, he was not sure he could find another job that he liked as much as this one, even with all the pressure, the tension, the long hours. He was deeply involved with the kids, particularly his own cases. In traditional psychotherapy, he had been told, you keep your distance; if you're the therapist, or the counselor, you never get emotionally entangled with your patients. But that was not how it worked at the Center. When he told a kid he loved him, or her, he meant it. Like the rest of the staff he depended on other people, who weren't so personally involved, to keep an objective eye on what was happening. With few exceptions, he ended up loving the kids who stayed around long enough—sometimes just long enough to hurt him when they left.

And then there was the matter of Betsy Coleman. Kevin had spent a couple of weekends in New Jersey with Margie, the schoolteacher. Margie was pretty, nice, amusing, willing, affectionate and probably wanted to marry him. Betsy was beautiful, intelligent, and—he had heard—dating a much older man with money.

Betsy walked into the staff office for the one o'clock meeting looking like something off the cover of a magazine. There was a rule that staff members might not wear jeans, a rule that annoyed most of the counselors but never bothered Betsy. She was always perfectly groomed, and even in simple clothes she looked like a model. One of the problems Kevin often had to deal with was that the boys who became his cases invariably at some point —if not from day one—had eyes for Betsy. The girls idolized her, and some of them ended up having eyes for her too.

He and Betsy were, Kevin believed, pretty good friends. They sometimes had weekend duty together, when the house was loose and the kids were playing games and listening to records. Then they grabbed a few minutes in the staff office, taking a break from the relentless talking and listening to eat their cheese and pastrami sandwiches and discuss something besides the kids. He was aware of their differences. She was much more verbal than he. She had been to a prestigious private college; he was barely scraping through a branch of the state university. And anyway, they weren't supposed to get involved with each other. So why was she on his mind all the time?

One of the things they talked about was their common interest: photography. Again she one-upped him. He had an old Minolta. She owned a Nikon with a bagful of lenses—telephoto, wide-angle, zoom. And a darkroom. When she went home, she had told him, she shut herself up in her darkroom to relax. He had an enlarger, but setting it up in Mrs. Bremen's cottage bathroom and then talking it down again got to be too much, especially with his schoolwork.

Yesterday he had made a move. There was an exhibit in New York he wanted to see. Would she like to drive in with him?

Yes, she had said, she would.

He wondered if they would have to report this to Paul Kendricks or Dr. Stone. He decided not. After all, they were just friends. And he didn't ask her about the man she was supposedly seeing.

In staff meeting Betsy said she was worried about David

Peterson. She told them she would bet her last dollar the kid had some kind of guilt—probably something that had happened when he was home. They all recognized the symptoms. "It's just a matter of time," Kevin commented. "He'll either cop to it, or he'll split. So I guess all you can do is keep up the pressure on him." They both wished the kid would admit whatever he'd done and get it over with.

"What do you think?"

She had been looking for an opportunity for three days to ask him—first when he came back from driving David and Doug to the Center on Sunday afternoon, then after dinner when Susie went down to the family room to watch televison, later after they went to bed and lay facing in opposite directions, *not* the next morning because Richard never liked to talk in the morning, but the next evening and the one after that. Finally she decided not to wait any longer.

"What do you think of Davey?"

Richard Peterson had been thinking of little else. He really could not understand anything about what was the matter with the boy. And he certainly did not understand what this Center was all about, or what it was they thought they were going to do for him there. When the situation had first come up, and it had become obvious they had to find some place, something, or somebody to help David before they all went crazy, the Center had seemed like the answer. At least *an* answer. Of course, he didn't pretend to know much about psychology or psychiatry or any of those things, but it seemed to him that what these kids needed most was some good old-fashioned discipline. A hard kick where it counted. His wife didn't approve of hitting children, but sometimes that was the only thing that had any effect, hurting them just enough so they knew they had to obey.

Richard did not expect David to be beaten at the Center; that, he firmly believed, should be in the hands of the parents. But he did think the boy needed to be taught a few good lessons. Instead, there was all that talk about peer pressure. Richard couldn't see that the kids could teach each other anything good. Weren't they all there for the same reason, because they hadn't learned to behave? And the counselors didn't look much older or even much different from the kids, except they all seemed to have beards. That Kevin Murphy seemed hardly old enough to know what he was doing, a boy himself. What could he be, twenty-four or five? Meanwhile, he was paying out all this money to have his son treated by a former junkie. And now there was a girl who looked like a movie star. It seemed ridiculous.

Dr. Stone, who ran the place, struck Richard as no better and probably no worse than any of the other headshrinkers he had met during all this business with David. He was, at least, an adult, but his ideas of getting all of them together, Susie and Richie, too, just to see how things worked in the family seemed completely off-base. Stone's idea was that each family had a unique kind of "dance," and if one person was out of step in the dance it threw the whole thing out of kilter. That person was elected unconsciously by the rest of the family to be the one who made the mistakes. The reason behind all this, Stone had explained to them in his office, was that often it was not just one person who was mixed-up, but the whole family. The kid was the "sick" one who called for help for everybody else. Dr. Stone believed that in most of the families he had met, the kid who wound up at the Center was only one part of the family that needed help. It was clear to Ricard that Stone thought the Petersons were one of those families.

Well, that was crazy. There was nothing wrong with the Petersons that getting David fixed up wouldn't cure. Richie was doing just fine, getting good grades, heading for a bright future. Susie was as cute as could be. He and Ellen never fought; never. Partly because of his iron self-control. He prided himself on never losing his temper except for that one time; in fact he had forgotten why it was he slapped her then. When they were first married and something went wrong, she would start to cry, but she had soon learned that it got her nowhere. As soon as she began to control herself, things had improved. Richard himself had not cried since he was sixteen and his mother had died, and he regarded tears as a sign of weakness. A woman might be able to cry, but not a man. In that way David was like him; he never cried when he was punished.

Richard didn't know what to say to Ellen about David now. You really couldn't tell much in one weekend, especially with that other kid around. He certainly hoped David would keep in mind that he was costing the family a lot of money, and that he would do his best to get straightened out as soon as possible. It would be the first time in a long while the boy would have done anything that pleased him.

"He seems to be doing okay," Richard answered his wife. "I guess that's as much as we can expect."

*Okay?* She thought she saw more than just okay. It was hard to judge with Doug along—a nice enough boy, but his table manners were dreadful; some parents just didn't bother with any kind of training—and there was never a chance for her and David to sit down and talk by themselves. He seemed nervous to her, worse on Sunday than on Saturday. It was almost as though he could hardly wait to leave, and she had planned all those goods meals for him and then wasn't sure he even enjoyed them. On Sunday he was tense and edgy. She thought maybe something had happened between him and his friend Doug. She wondered when he would come home again, and she thought of

82

calling Betsy to ask if there were any problems. Something told her something was wrong.

The whole time David was there she had kept remembering what Dr. Stone had to say about the family dance, that they somehow had picked David to be the one who was out of step, to show them that something was wrong with the whole family. It scared her when she thought about it, because it forced her to go on and think about other things: what was wrong with *her* perhaps. Maybe what was wrong was her and Richard. And she knew there was no way to change that. What would happen, she wondered, when David got better and came home to live? He wouldn't be out of step any more, and if there was still something wrong with the dance pattern in the family, all the problems would crop up somewhere else. Maybe Richie. Maybe Susie. Maybe herself. When she realized all that might happen to them, she began to cry. Quietly, though; Richard hated it when she cried, so it always had to be in secret.

Wednesday afternoon she phoned Betsy, who said she was glad for the call. How had the weekend gone? Fine, Ellen said. Betsy didn't quite believe her. Had anything gone wrong? No, everything had been fine, it was wonderful to see David, she felt he was making wonderful progress. But she was just sort of curious to hear from Betsy how she thought he was doing.

Betsy picked up a lot of anxiety from the call, but she wasn't sure exactly what it was about. What had gone wrong? Ellen didn't say, either wouldn't or couldn't, and Betsy hadn't pressed. But afterwards Betsy wondered if she should have forced the issue. Maybe Mrs. Peterson sensed something and didn't want to say unless it was pulled out of her. Parents! It was tough enough working with the kids, but she sometimes had the feeling it was the parents who should be at the Center, learning to express their feelings and going through changes, instead of the kids.

The poor kids. Poor David. What was going on there? Betsy knew she would have to wait to find out.

It took another ten days. Every time David managed to forget, something pulled his mind back again, and his torment increased. He was miserable. The guilt chewed relentlessly at him, and he brooded about quitting. Yet something held him. Finally he went to Jay and in three sentences gave him the whole story. He was trembling. Jay put his arm across his shoulders. "You tell staff yet?"

"Not yet. I don't know how."

"If you don't, I have to."

"I know. I can't. You tell them."

David waited, smoking one cigarette after another, knowing he, not Jay, should have gone to staff. Then word came from Paul Kendricks that he was wanted in the staff office. Betsy was there, too, and Kevin and some others.

They blew him away: he was an idiot, a baby, an asshole. They had reason enough to throw him right out of the Center. He knew that. Did he want to stay? He nodded. He understood they'd make it rough for him. He'd have to get his hair cut, have to face the family and apologize, lose his job function, get a hookup. He knew all that. Kevin pulled out the shears and chopped off about an inch of David's bushy brown hair.

That afternoon they put him in a group. Jay was there, and Doug, and some other people he was close to. "Why did you do it?" they demanded. "What made you sneak out like that, with your friend Doug sleeping right there in the same room, and go off with those shits? Don't you realize how you hurt your friends here when you do a dumb thing like that? How stupid can you get? You act like a real asshole! Who are those guys anyway? What have they ever done for you? Nothing but get you in trouble! But you sneak out with them! You're tight with Doug, right? Well, look at him! Look at his face!"

With tremendous effort David pulled his eyes up to Doug's face. Doug was crying silently.

"Look how you're hurting him! This is your friend, he cares about you, and you're hurting him like this. And look at Jay! You told Jay you love him, and look what you're doing to him."

Tears stood in Jay's eyes, his emotions were peeled raw and open. Then David felt his own face begin to crumple, and the pain and fear came welling up. "How does it make you feel that you hurt people like this, Dave! Your friends, Dave! Dave, *look at them*! How does it make you feel?"

"Like shit!" he wailed.

"Keep talking," they yelled at him, calling to him at the bottom of the pit of self-disgust where he had slid. "Keep talking about what it feels like to hurt people like this. Keep talking about how it feels to be a shit, a real asshole!"

"It hurts," he moaned. "Oh God, it hurts! I didn't want to hurt them, I didn't want to . . . but I did. Oh God, Jay, Doug . . . I'm sorry I hurt you . . . I didn't want to. . . ."

"So why did you do it then? Does it make you feel like a man to sneak out with some guys who don't give a shit for you, to go drink beer with them? Is that what makes you feel like a man?"

"I don't know, nothing seemed to be going right . . . my father was complaining about me, my brother's getting high, my sister, she's heading into something like this, maybe the wrong direction, maybe it's because of me, I don't know. . . . My father doesn't see that I'm changing, he's still on my back, still thinks I'm a fuck-up. I want him to love me! I want my father to love me!" Despair flooded through him, and the cry came out like a wail.

"Let it out, Dave," they said, one voice after another, a

gentle, coaxing chorus now. "Let it come, Dave. Tell us how it hurts, how it feels to know your father doesn't love you."

"It hurts . . . I feel so lonely . . . such a shit. . . ." With relief he let go of it, the guilt and the longing. He did not know there was so much bottled up in him. He started to tell them, half sobbing, gasping for breath, about how Richie was the favorite, always had been, and then Susie, everybody but him, they didn't ever love him, his mother maybe, but even she loved Richie more.

"Keep talking," they coaxed. And he did. He realized then that he was crying in front of all these people, and it was all right. When he had first come to the Center he had promised himself he would never cry in a group. They'd never get him to do that, ever. But he had learned to trust them enough to let it happen.

"I know how you feel, Dave." Doug's face came into focus gradually, through the swell of tears, and his voice emerged from the chorus. "I don't even know who my real father *is*. And my stepfather, he hasn't hardly even looked at me since he married my mother and they started having kids of their own. Sometimes when he's drunk he says, 'You ain't even my son! You nothing but a bastard nobody wanted!' So I know how it feels, Dave. I know how you're hurting."

"Maybe you're going to have to live with this for a while, Dave." It was Betsy somewhere off to his left, her voice level and kind. "Maybe you're going to have to give your father some time to see how you're changing. Maybe he'll change, too. But maybe he won't. Maybe he can't, even if he wants to. But that, in the long run, has nothing to do with you. It's your life, Dave. And if you're going to run off with negative friends, people who aren't ever going to have one fraction of the loyalty of the friends you have here, just because of something stupid your father, or anybody else, says to you, then you're not making much

86

progress here. You understand that? You're responsible for your own life, and you've got to do what's right for yourself."

He nodded dumbly, too exhausted to speak. But that was not the end of it.

"All right, now you're going to have to go in front of the family this evening and apologize. And then you're hooked up to bathrooms. You just start mopping down the bathroom walls, floors, toilets, sinks, and when you get that finished you start all over again. When you want a break, you ask staff. And you tell staff when you had your last break and how long it lasted. Is that clear?"

A few hours later David stood up in front of all the ORs and Intermediates collected in the dining room and a couple of Phase-Outs who happened to be around although it was one of their off nights and told them he was sorry. Betsy interrupted. "Tell them exactly what you did, David."

He recited the whole story over again. Those who had not been in the group earlier yelled at him just the way the group had. He was humiliated at having to go through this, and he cried again from the embarrassment, but the pain he had gone through this afternoon had disappeared, drained out of him.

For the next three weeks, David scrubbed white tile and porcelain until he thought he would go up the wall. His hair grew. He went through more changes.

But he still was not allowed to go home for Christmas. His mother called and said they were all going to his grandmother's in Hartford, as they did every year. It was the first year that he wouldn't be with them. He thought of Grandma, his mother's mother. He had an idea she loved him best, certainly in his immediate family and maybe even among all eight of his cousins. She wouldn't ever tell him that, of course, but he knew. There was a time when he wished he could go live with her. He still thought of that sometimes, but when they had let him go there alone for a whole week during the summer, he had blown it—he took some money from her purse. She had caught him and bawled him out. She had trusted him, she had said, and he had betrayed her; she loved him, but she would not have a thief in the house. And she sent him home to his parents again. He felt sorry about that now. And he wished he could be with her for Christmas.

Everybody seemed to be going somewhere, although when it came right down to it, there were about twenty-five of them left at the Center. A couple of mothers came in to help Kevin, who had pulled early duty for that day and was in charge of the kitchen since Fred had the day off. They produced a huge meal —baked ham, roast turkey, yams, mashed potatoes, the works. Lots of parents sent in desserts, so there were cakes and pies and cookies until he couldn't cram down another mouthful. It was a terrific meal but one hell of a day to be hooked up to the dishpan. For once David was thankful to be on bathrooms.

CHAPTER 4

GLITTERY ICICLES DROOPED OUTSIDE THE CLASSROOM WINDOW, and the late winter sun glared on the fresh snow. Ted Valentine had promised to take some of them cross-country skiing the next time it snowed like this. With difficulty David dragged his attention away from a fantasy of gliding through a white forest and back to Mrs. Talmadge, who was lecturing the four members of the class about Africa. Very little skiing there, David suspected. He could scarcely keep his mind on what she was saying. Algebra was better. Sister Mary Francis taught that class. She dressed in a pants suit and her almost-white hair was done in a beauty parlor. But she wore a big cross on a chain around her neck, which showed she was a nun.

The Center rented classrooms in a former Catholic parochial school. Every morning at a quarter of eight, Jim Dahl collected the students in the van and drove them two miles up Old Ridge Road to the school, and at noon he picked them up and brought them back to the Center in time for lunch. It really wasn't bad —three classes in the morning, only a handful of kids in each class, no homework since they had to do all the work during class. Better than regular school ever was.

When David first came to the Center they had given him all kinds of reading and math tests. He had had lots of tests done on him when he was in public school too, and his guidance counselor had said he was above average in intelligence, probably college material if he wanted to go. He didn't know what he wanted to do. There was a time when he was much younger and had wanted to be a racing car driver. A litte later, while still in his car phase, he had gotten interested in mechanics. Sometimes he thought he'd like to be a heart surgeon. They made lots of money. His mother was pleased when he talked about going into medicine because of being a trained nurse herself. In fact she was talking about going back to work again, now that everybody was practically grown. His father was still opposed to it, even though he said they needed the money. When David was home last, his father had complained about how much it cost for him to be at the Center. He said, trying to make it sound like a joke, "If you had been paroled there, the state would've paid for it. We should have let you get arrested again. They'd never have let you off a second time."

When he was taking the tests, David had spent a long time talking with Mrs. Aldrich, the director of education for the Center. She had asked him what he was interested in, and he had told her his two ideas: car mechanic and heart surgeon. "It sounds as though you like to fix things," she said. He had never thought of it that way, but he guessed it might be so. Soon after he had made Intermediates, Mrs. Aldrich had told him he could start attending classes.

School was going fairly well. He got along with the teachers, liked math, struggled with English, tolerated social studies. He could hardly remember any more what it was like to sit in a huge class of thirty-some people, goofing off in the back row, never paying attention, just waiting for the teacher to turn her back so he could flash a message to one of his buddies. He used to frustrate the daylights out of the teachers. It was hard for them to believe he could pay so little attention in class—when he bothered to go at all—and still manage to pass the tests. Actually his test grades weren't that bad, but he never handed in any homework. And his attitude was negative, to put it mildly.

He didn't know yet if he would be able to make up the time he had lost. Ninth grade was a total disaster. He passed everything, but just barely: mostly D's, a couple of C's. His mother had cried when she saw the report card. When he was a little kid, in the first few grades, he had been such a good student—mostly A's, sometimes a B. Then in sixth grade, when he moved to the middle school, things had started to go wrong, and from then on it was downhill. He could see now that it must have driven his parents crazy.

Not just the grades. They didn't know at first all the things he was doing. By the time he was eleven, he was smoking a lot of cigarettes. He was thirteen when he first got high and started trying other things, like pills and some glue-sniffing. Skipping school, hanging out at the Pizza Palace and taking a few things, like records and cigarettes, just for kicks. That was when he and Billy had started cruising around together a lot. Billy was one of those kids who could come into your home and charm your parents. He shook hands with your father and talked the way adults like. His English was perfect, his manners were smooth, he acted interested in grown-up subjects, always with this gentlemanly smile on his face. He never swore, even accidentally. This was different from other guys, like Tony, who were always sort of the same, no matter where you ran into them. Naturally David's parents liked Billy. "Bring him here any time you want. He's like one of the family."

They didn't know the real Billy, of course. They didn't know it was Billy who started him getting high or showed him how to walk into a store with an air that made the clerks and manager *trust* him. He had that wonderful way of acting around adults that David tried to imitate but never learned to do even half as well as Billy. If you had Billy along you didn't have to know how—he could pull it off for both of you. It wasn't until Billy got the motorcycle that David's parents began to catch on that maybe Billy wasn't quite so perfect as they had thought. It was hard for them to imagine that anybody who said please and thank you and may I and pardon me as much as Billy did could be anything but good.

By the time David was fourteen—Billy was a year older and the bike was a gift from Billy's father who didn't care that it was illegal—they knew, but then it was too late. There was nothing they could do. Lock him up in his room? There were too many ways to get out. He had learned from Billy how to look really *sorry* for whatever it was they found out he had done, and how to make it appear that he was trying hard to shape up. Then the two of them would get together and laugh their butts off at how they had put something over on the old farts.

In ninth grade David's guidance counselor told him that he

had a reading problem. David had reported that to Billy, who said, "I'll get you something to help that," and soon presented him with a collection of pornographic magazines. "If you can't read, you can at least look at the pictures," Billy had advised. They laughed themselves silly over that one. Not that he hadn't seen these magazines before. He had discovered his father's secret collection of *Playboy* when he was about eight, and he routinely checked Richie's room, but he had never really looked at anything quite so gross as the magazines Billy had stolen to help his reading problem.

Even as they had rolled on the floor whooping and hollering and yelling, "Sick! This is the sickest thing I've ever seen in my life!" it had turned them on. And that's when it had happened for the first time, between the two of them. Afterward David was frightened, really scared. But Billy told him not to worry. They were best friends, weren't they? They would swear never to tell another soul. Swear it in blood!

They did it often after that. It worried David a lot, even though Billy kept reassuring him that it didn't mean he was really queer. Once when he had heard his father ranting about homosexuals not being part of the human race and saying fairies should not be allowed to have jobs where they could pollute the young, David had been terrified that his father would somehow find out. The next time he had been with Billy he had said he wouldn't do it any more. Then Billy had gotten mad and said if he didn't do it he'd make sure everybody, especially Mr. Peterson, found out that David was queer. And that had frightened David more than ever. Then Billy had started to cry and said David was the best friend he had ever had.

When Mrs. Aldrich talked to him about his reading problem, David couldn't help but think of Billy and the skin magazines, and the memory always made him nervous. She was very patient with him. "Look, there are all kinds of ways to learn things. Some people learn best by hearing, others have to see something done. Some people have to read it or repeat the instructions out loud or in writing. And some people have to use combinations of these things. Everybody has certain strengths and certain weaknesses. For instance, if you were to tell me how to get to your house, I wouldn't be able to remember the directions. But if you drew me a map, I could remember it after I looked at it and got the picture in my mind. It doesn't mean you're stupid, Dave. It just means you have to try to develop other ways of learning things, and we have to figure out the ways you learn best."

But that wasn't what he was nervous about.

Starting classes at the Center School after he made Intermediates had been a big change for David—one of several. Through most of the winter he kept his job function on kitchen crew. Mostly he worked on food preparation. Occasionally he was in charge of calling the tables, one at a time to keep the line moving smoothly past the serving counter but not letting it get too long. Sometimes he was behind the counter, ladling out the pieces of chicken or the spaghetti and sauce. When he noticed that one of the girls wasn't eating enough, he pulled her up: "You got to eat something. A little bit of everything," he advised. "It's not good for you to skip meals." And he encouraged the people who were on reducing diets, too.

Then they transferred him to communications. Somebody decided he had a flair for drawing and lettering, and he found himself in charge of creating giant-sized birthday cards, which everybody signed, for staff members and of making sure there was a supply of mimeographed forms. Dozens of them. At the front desk, where an expediter was on duty in the afternoons and evenings, there was a whole batch of forms. Everybody signed in and out every day. If you were going some place special, like the dentist, you had to sign a separate sheet for that. There was still another sheet for keeping track of staff, so the expediters could find somebody if he or she were needed. And every hour one of the expediters went around and did a check of every member in the program to make sure he or she was where he or she was supposed to be and filled out a form. Mostly one of the girls did the typing and David ran the mimeo machine.

He missed the kitchen and hated this job. He could complain, of course. They would tell him that doing a job he didn't like was a learning experience. That life was full of jobs people didn't like to do, and one of the changes he and everybody else in the program had to go through was learning to stick to a job that wasn't particularly pleasant. Besides, it was better than being assigned to the laundry room with leftover socks and fuzz in the machines.

He wondered if he would ever be an expediter, running around in a necktie with a notebook in his hip pocket, being responsible, keeping an eye out for everything that was going on. It seemed a long way off.

David was not the only one those life was changing. After a couple of years of working with ORs, Kevin had been switched to counseling Intermediates, and many of his former OR cases, including David Peterson, had been reassigned to him. Now Kevin and Betsy were working with the same bunch of kids in their Tuesday and Thursday night groups, and they spent more time together comparing notes.

Their styles were completely different, both personally and professionally. Kevin allowed himself to get angry at the kids— it was part of being involved with them—to shout at them in groups, to administer roaring verbal haircuts when the situation warranted.

Betsy kept her approach on a lower key. She was firm, but she rarely raised her voice. Sometimes she wondered if all the fireworks and bombast were really necessary. Most of the staff members were male, and stridently *macho* at that. That was fine for some of the tough boys who came into the Center, but she questioned if the more sensitive boys and most of the girls really needed or could respond to the kind of verbal abuse that was sometimes poured on them. Betsy did not intend to argue the point; whatever they did individually seemed to work. But Betsy was a feminist, and feminism had a bad time surviving at the Center. She used to think that boys and girls were born the same and that it was their parents and others in the widening circle of their lives who molded them into such strikingly different types. She was no longer so sure about that.

The girls were manipulators, each and every one of them. Betsy could not think of a single girl who had come through the Center since she had been there who hadn't used tears or flirtatiousness or some other angle for getting what she wanted. The boys were far more straightforward. When a new boy came into the program, the older member boys were quick to pull him in. But the girls took their time with a new girl, jealously checking out the size of her bosom, the condition of her skin, the style of her clothes. She remembered the day Carla MacLoughlin arrived, a real beauty and a big threat to some of the other girls, many of whom were also exceptionally pretty. They ignored her for days. The boys *never* gave a hard time to a new boy just because he was good looking.

The girls got away with too much, Betsy felt. There was a double standard right down the line, and some of these spoiled little princesses could have been brought around much faster if that standard were replaced with something more equitable. There were no physical haircuts for girls, for instance. Betsy didn't necessarily think there should be, but she did believe walking around for a few weeks with an ugly stocking pulled over their hair might be an effective alternative.

Meanwhile, Betsy was getting closer to Kevin Murphy. She didn't quite know how to handle this attraction. She wasn't at all sure she was ready for another serious relationship; she was still wary from the last one. Also, there was the Center's brother-and-sister rule. But Kevin seemed to have many of the qualities she was looking for in a man—when she looked. For a long time they had seen each other casually around the Center. Then they got in the habit of stopping for coffee on their way home from work, and once they went out for a beer. Conversation was mainly about their cases.

Things had stayed light and friendly between them until they discovered their mutual passion for photography and spent a day in New York together seeing as many exhibits as they could track down. They didn't talk about the Center then, or the kids, or even much about the pictures. They began to talk about themselves and got around to acknowledging the attraction that existed between them. Kevin wanted to go to Dr. Stone then and there and tell him they wanted to begin going together. Betsy reasoned that the answer would certainly be no. And if the answer was no, one of them would have to give up the job, and neither wanted to do that. Or, if the answer was yes and they started dating and it didn't work out, it would be embarrassing and very hard to keep on working together. "Let's just let it go for a while," Betsy suggested. "Just see each other around the Center for a few months and find out what happens. No sense in getting everybody in an uproar for nothing." She was testing her own feelings, buying herself some time.

Patience was not Kevin's special virtue, not in matters like this, but there wasn't much he could do. So he agreed to Betsy's plan, to do nothing.

The sweater David's grandmother sent for Christmas triggered the blowup. He wasn't sure he liked the sweater, mostly because he hadn't seen anyone else wearing anything like it, red with a kind of white snowflake pattern knitted across the front. They each got one—Richie's was blue and green, Susie's pink and white. David didn't wear his until one very cold day when he was going to be outside and wearing a jacket over it most of the time anyway, so he decided to try it. If anybody said a word, he'd take it off and that would be that.

It was a snotty new kid, all mouth and heading for trouble. "Hey, look at that *sweater*," the boy lisped, flipping a limp wrist at David. "If you don't look just good enough to *eat*, sweetie!"

David felt hot blood rising through his neck and into his face. He wanted to smash the kid, bloody his punk face. He did not. He told the kid to knock it off, said he was going to take him to a group about it. But the kid didn't quit. Seething, David yanked off the sweater as soon as he got to his room and put it under all his other clothes in a bureau drawer. But twice more that day he saw the kid, and each time the kid didn't say a word—just held up his wrist and tossed his head or dropped a lewd wink. The third time the rage boiled over and David shoved the kid hard against the wall. "Not one more time," he said, "or you're going to be spitting out those squirrely teeth of yours."

And somebody saw him. Fifteen minutes later he was in the front office, and Paul and Ted Valentine were all over him. He knew the rules—no physical violence of any kind. What was he coming off his belly like that for, anyway? David tried to explain.

"You don't know better than that? How long you been here now? Five months? Almost six! And somebody says something that bothers you and you don't have sense enough to take him to a group? Jeez, who ever let you out of OR!"

Paul turned to the punky kid and burned him, too. "And what's *your* problem? In my experience, it's the kid who accuses somebody else of being queer who has a lot of problems himself. We call that projecting. And Dave! There must be some reason you let yourself get carried away like that. This is the first time you got physical with anybody, right? Maybe you ought to talk to Kevin about this. Meanwhile, you're hooked up to the pan."

The dishpan again. He couldn't believe it. He'd only been off bathrooms for six weeks. Later that afternoon he slumped in the chair next to Kevin's desk.

"What's with you, Dave? What're you letting yourself get upset by that little creep for?"

"He thinks I'm queer. He made a couple of remarks about a sweater I had on this morning, and then he keeps giving me that lah-dee-dah crap. I hate his guts."

"So you hate his guts, but you know better than to go around slamming people against walls. That really get you so upset?"

"Yeah."

"Something tells me maybe you and Billy had something going more than a couple of times. Am I right? And that you're pretty scared you might really be homosexual after all. Right again?"

"Yes, I guess so."

"You *guess* so! Time for you to talk to Charlie."

Charlie Toth was the house specialist in sexuality. There was, as Charlie said, very little he didn't know about the subject from first-hand experience, and his frankness was his way of getting the boys to open up about their feelings.

"When I was your age," Charlie informed David while they sat across from each other in the Intermediate office, "I was living out in L.A., hanging around the bus depot, going home with anybody who'd give me money for my next fix. For a while I stayed with a jazz drummer, and he shared me with his band

and their friends. One big scummy family, you know? Then the drummer got busted and I had a fight with the band and started drifting east, hitting all the bus stations along the way."

By some miracle, Charlie wound up at the Center, managed to kick the drugs, and decide to be straight. "Then I found out it wasn't women I had been hating all that time, it was *me* I hated. When I started feeling pretty good about myself, I started feeling pretty good about girls, too. I got to know some girls, and I made friends with them, and I tried to find out what they were like. Then I fell in love with one who had been my friend. She knew everything there was to know about me, and she still loved me. We got married five years ago." Charlie displayed a photograph of his family, Louise and their two children, plus a boy from her former marriage. Louise had large dark eyes and crinkly hair and was pretty enough so that the boys in Charlie's groups admired her and envied him.

Every couple of weeks Charlie gathered some of the boys for a sexuality group, and Yvonne Frey took the girls. Yvonne's background was not so colorful as Charlie's, but she let the girls know that she had had sex with at least a dozen different boys before she was fourteen. There was nothing they could say that would shock her.

David could not get his head straightened out. There were times when he thought about Billy with a mixture of longing and revulsion. There were times when he thought about other guys in the program, confirming his worst fears about himself. Other times, when the girls strode by in jeans that fitted tight, he thought he'd go out of his head. There were times when David thought of practically nothing but sex.

Then he found out everybody else did too. Charlie kept hammering at them: they're all your brothers and sisters. Your feelings are normal, but you have to control them. So you don't set up any situations. Boys and girls use the laundry room on different days; it's too easy to be alone there. When you sit on the sofa in the living room, a guy doesn't flop down between two girls and vice versa. You're never alone with a girl. But you don't run away from the situation and just have guys as friends either. That's not normal. So you get to know each other, like brothers and sisters. It's a family, remember? You get to be friends with girls, if you're a guy, and you find out what they're like, what they think like, how they expect to be treated. So that when you're ready to make friends on the outside and start dating, you got some idea of what you're doing. Sometimes you'll decide that you're really getting close to a girl in the program, and you'll want to tell her you love her. But you and staff better be damned sure you're not thinking from the waist down—that it's real friendship.

But when you find that you've got eyes for somebody, male or female, that you're attracted sexually, then you have to stay clear of that person until you're sure it's under control. You tell staff about it. You talk about it in groups and on the floor. You don't let it run you. You jerk off.

David was still wrestling with his worries about being queer when he admitted to himself that he had eyes for Carla MacLoughlin. Carla had come into the program a few weeks before David, and they had been in a lot of groups together since. Carla had spectacular blue eyes with long eyelashes, clear skin, and a round figure. She claimed that she didn't like her chin, which had a large dimple in it. She had a way of tossing her long blond hair and a habit of combing it incessantly that he had noticed the first night he was at the Center and they had played the word game. When she had first come into the program she had worn the same tight sweater and jeans day after day, but after she became an Intermediate she switched to skirts and blouses.

One night after dinner during the regular meeting, Betsy

asked Carla to stand up and said, "I hear you've been wondering when you're going to make Intermediates." David, sitting near Carla, saw her swallow and blush. "What makes you think you're ready to be an Intermediate, Carla?" Betsy pressed.

He saw her twist the comb in her hands. "I think I've learned a lot about being honest," she said in a faint voice. "And I think I'm really getting more responsible for myself."

"Okay, then," Betsy announced smiling. "You're an Intermediate, Carla."

Everyone applauded and Carla's friends squealed and jumped up to hug her. She blushed, as usual.

David knew a lot about Carla. He had sat through enough groups with her to know her story, and what he hadn't learned in groups he had found out talking to her on the floor—at meal times, in the living room after dinner. She had several brothers and sisters. Her real father had deserted when she was a little baby, leaving her mother alone with Carla and her older sister. Then her mother married again and had four more children. The new husband was an alcoholic. Once when he was drunk he raped Carla's older sister. Carla hated him for that. The sister had run away, and Carla missed her. If it hadn't been for the stepfather, she would never have run away. After that, Carla was always afraid he might come after her. She told him she would kill him if he tried. When that marriage fell apart, her mother had a nervous breakdown. Then she had recovered and had moved in with her new boyfriend, a man ten years younger than she was and twelve years older than Carla. For a while Clara slept with him. Then her mother had found out, they had a terrible fight, and Carla had run away. She had wanted to go live with her sister, but the sister never even answered Carla's letters.

So she had started going with guys, whoever would have her. She drank a lot and got high almost every day. She was arrested several times as a runaway, a status offense that got her sent to a detention home for a while. Carla was something of an expert on all the possible places a juvenile offender could be sent: Starkweather, group homes, detention homes—she'd been to all of them. Wherever they sent her, she ran away. Finally, the last time, she was made a ward of the state and packed off to the Center. She wore long sleeves to hide the tattoos on her arms, the initials of some of the boys she had been to bed with. She wanted to get rid of the marks, but she didn't know how. So, long sleeves.

Sometimes Carla got very depressed. In groups she admitted to thoughts about life on the outside, and she wondered what had happened to all the boys she used to run around with. They all had loved her—they told her so. When she got very depressed she sometimes cut her wrists, but never deeply enough to be really dangerous. Before she had come to the Center, she had thought a lot about dying, and she still talked about it sometimes.

David remembered being in the art therapy group with her. She was the one who had been afraid to shut her eyes.

With all those troubles, Carla appeared to be doing better than David. It seemed she never broke a rule, never acted out her feelings. Smoking in the dining room one day after dinner, she told him, "I've had enough shit to last a lifetime. This is the last stop for me. If I don't make it here, I'll never make it anywhere."

He watched her, full of admiration. And, sometimes, full of desire.

He couldn't bear to admit that he had eyes for her, that he sometimes tried to look down the neck of her long-sleeved blouse to catch a glimpse of the curve of her breasts. If he admitted that he had eyes for her, they would be put on the ban, and he would not allowed to talk to her. He didn't want that to happen, so he tried to stop the sexual thoughts. It didn't work.

In Kevin's Intermediate group one day, one of Carla's friends accused her of having eyes for Jay. She denied it. They kept at her. She had a reputation as the "house flirt." When was she going to get over it? David found himself joining in the confrontation, suddenly jealous that if she was going to have eyes for anybody it was for Jay and not for him. Why was she always hanging around him, then? She began to cry—she was one who cried easily—and finally admitted it.

David, angry at her and at the same time wanting to comfort her, brought her a tissue. His reaction did not go unnoticed. "You came down pretty hard on Carla just now, Dave," Kevin remarked. "Why is that?"

He started to deny it. He just wasn't ready to say anything. He was still hooked up to the dishpan for shoving the creepy kid, and damned if he was going to get into trouble again. He'd never get out of the hookup. This was something he was sure he could handle himself.

"I think you're projecting, Dave. I think you've got eyes for somebody yourself. Maybe for Carla. You're pretty close to her, aren't you?"

"Yeah, we're good friends. But that's it, Kevin, honest."

*Honest.*

Staff wanted him to try another weekend at home. He said he didn't want to go. This was his family, here at the Center.

"You're scared aren't you?" Betsy asked him in a group.

Yes. Not of running into Billy; he was sure he could handle that this time. But he wasn't sure he could handle his mother and father and Richie and Susie.

"It's important for you to go, Dave. One of the things you're here to learn to do is to get along with your family out there. Some day, believe it or not, you'll be leaving here and going home to live. And you have to know those people, to let them get to know you, to see how you're changing. Dave, it's not easy. But you have to try."

He took Jay along for strength.

"The kids at school all say the Center is for creeps and faggots," Susie announced while they were building a fire in the family room fireplace.

"Well, it's not. It's a good place. We're all there trying to help each other change." He could hardly believe he was saying this, remembering how he had felt a few months ago.

"Are *you* changing, Davey?"

"I think so. Do I seem any different to you?"

"Yeah, I guess so." She studied him for a moment. "You used to be really with it. Now you're so straight it's revolting." She made a face and ran off.

David coaxed a flame under the kindling. He didn't like what was happening to Susie. He knew some of the kids she hung out with, and he didn't much like them either. The boys were older, and most of them got high or drank. Probably Susie was getting high, too. Maybe even popping pills. The phone rang constantly for her; her end of the conversation was always guarded, almost as though she were talking in code. Just like he used to be at her age. He cornered her again later that day, dreading the confrontation. "Susie, you been getting high?"

She laughed in his face and whirled away. "Are you kidding? And end up in a place like you did? Not me, brother. But I'll tell you something." She came up close to him and looked him straight in the eye. "If I ever do, I'll know how to handle it. I won't get into trouble the way you did. That was stupid. I'm not stupid."

A confession that was not a confession. He didn't know what to do next. She sure wouldn't listen to anything he had to say. Would he have listened to anybody? Hell no! Maybe she'd listen to Richie, except Richie was getting high, too. Talk to his parents about it? Not his father, certainly. His father would figure David was just bad-rapping his little Susie to make himself look good. No point in that. And if he told his mother, and she believed him, what could she do about it? He discussed the situation with Jay. "We'll both talk to Susie," Jay said confidently.

What a stupid idea that turned out be! They told her they both knew that getting high was great. Everybody wanted to get high. The trouble was, most kids couldn't handle it, even when they thought they could. It was not physically addictive, like heroin and other drugs. But it got so you almost had to be high all the time, just to stay loose. And then you weren't doing much else with your life. Pretty soon then you needed money to buy grass, more than you could afford out of your allowance. So you probably started doing some stealing—money from your mother's purse, shoplifting a few things here and there. And then that got to be a habit, too, another kind of thrill. Getting high was more fun than going to school, and then school got to be a drag unless you could stay high there too, and your grades started going down and you hardly ever went any more. And the kids you started hanging out with were probably not the best kind either.

David could see that Susie would soon be getting involved with guys, going to bed with them, lots of them, like some of the girls at the Center. Lika Carla. She had been just about Susie's age when she had started screwing around. The thought made him sick in his stomach. He didn't expect Susie to listen to anything they told her, even though they were careful not to make it sound as though they were trying to preach at her.

"You guys are really full of it, you know that?" That's all she said when they had finished.

Maybe they could convince Richie to talk to her, even if he

didn't agree with them about getting high for himself. Just because of her age, if nothing else. But they never got around to that approach.

Richie went out early, right after dinner on Saturday, when the first flakes of a fresh snowfall were starting to float down. He took his father's car, promised to be in early. By ten o'clock a full-scale blizzard was in progress with an accumulation of five inches and at least five more predicted. The tension made everybody quiet. Ellen Peterson poked at some needlework. Richard Peterson sucked steadily on his pipe, restlessly shuffling the pages of a magazine he had already read, bored with whatever was on television. But he would not admit he was worried about Richie.

"He's driven in snow before," he said gruffly.

At midnight Ellen and Richard went upstairs to bed. Jay and David stayed in the family room to watch the late movie. The phone rang, a harsh, startling sound, and David picked it up just as his father answered in the bedroom. It was Richie. He had been in an accident. He wasn't hurt, but the car was totaled. And he was being held on a drunk driving charge.

Nobody got any sleep that night except Susie who wasn't wakened by the phone call. They decided to let Richie stay overnight at the station. Richard didn't know any lawyer he could call at that ungodly hour anyway and he couldn't see any point in going out in the blizzard. Besides, a night in a cell might teach him a lesson.

The next morning, though, they got Richie out on bail. And all hell broke loose. Richard raged at his oldest son. Then Ellen intervened. "Shouldn't we be thankful," she asked quaveringly, "that he's all right? Nobody was hurt, the car is insured. Certainly he has done a stupid thing to drink so much beer, but that could happen, couldn't it?"

Richard, infuriated, said to her bitterly, "If you could ever, just once, stop babying these kids, maybe they'd have a chance to grow up to be *men*. You've raised a drunk and a pothead," he roared at her. "You've spoiled them rotten. One in a loony bin, one in jail." On the other hand, he, of course, had nothing better to do than to work himself into a nervous breakdown or a heart attack or an ulcer trying to finance all this craziness. Money for the Center, now money for a lawyer! Was there no end to it? And what had he, Richard Peterson, done to deserve such a family? He had worked hard all his life, struggling up through the company, putting in hours of unpaid overtime, kissing asses left and right, just so he could give his family a decent life. This recital was followed by a rerun of his miserable boyhood, growing up blind poor, crammed together in a dinky house on the edge of nothing, often without decent clothes to go to school in, and so on. Yet somehow they had managed to produce three spoiled brats.

Susie had heard enough. She shot him a look of pure hatred. "Don't include me in your lineup, Dad," she said in a flat voice.

Furious, he spun around, his hand whipped out, there was a crack, a stunned gasp from Susie as the mark of the slap spread across her cheek, and a stifled scream from Ellen Peterson.

"Have you gone out of your mind, Richard? After all we've been through with the boys, you slap this child for one remark?"

It was the first time David could remember a family fight in which he was not the cause of and the magnet for all the anger. This time he was on the fringes, and from that safer distance he saw that his father wasn't angry at Susie and Richie so much as he was at their mother. That was really what this was all about: the kids were just chess pieces, and the adults were fighting through them. But did they fight like this when he wasn't around? And what was happening when they weren't fighting? He tried to recall what it was like before he had started getting into trouble. There was none of this fighting then, he was quite sure. Then he tried to remember if he had ever seen them hugging and kissing. He could not.

Even though the roads were slippery, Ellen Peterson insisted on going to the Monday night Parents Group. It was her turn to bring the dessert, and she made a large sponge cake, which she had packed into a carton and set on the seat beside her. Though Richard would still have nothing to do with the Parents Group, for Ellen it had become something to look forward to each week. Sometimes it was the only thing, the point from which she measured the days until the next one.

She now knew everyone in the organization fairly well, enough to be comfortable. Actually there weren't very many members. In the early days of the Center, when most of the children came from Greenfield itself or one of the towns around it, the group had been much larger. Now there were children being admitted from all over the state, and some of them even from out of state, and their parents obviously couldn't attend weekly meetings. Also many parents simply weren't interested. Like Richard. He couldn't see how it would help anybody if he went. If she wanted to, she could go. One from the family was enough anyway. He never asked what went on, and she didn't volunteer the information.

After coffee and cake and a short business meeting, they split up into small groups, husbands and wives in separate groups. At first Ellen felt very uncomfortable with all those people sitting and talking, not only about their children—that was what she expected it to be—but also about their own lives as well. Some of them were divorced and trying to bring up their children on their own. Some were unhappy in their marriages. One woman startled them all one evening with the long and tearful story of her extramarital affair. Not everybody in the group still had children at the Center. The woman who led Ellen's group had a son who had graduated from the program two years before. And there was another woman whose son had split and wound up in a lot of trouble again.

The people in the group were sympathetic. The leader always made sure they talked about how they *felt* about their problems, instead of what they *thought*. "Trust your feelings," Helen Majerski kept reminding them. "Your head can give you all sorts of false directions, but your feelings never lie. That's one thing our kids are learning, and we have to learn it too."

Ellen decided to tell them about Richie's accident with the car two nights ago. Everyone murmured sympathetically, and then someone asked, "How did your husband react?"

"He got angry and upset."

Someone else asked, "How did you feel about his reaction?"

It was as though something let go inside her. She began to weep softly and then to sob, deep heaving gasps that came up out of the lowest levels of her spirit. She heard herself saying something that she had not even allowed herself to think: "We don't have much of a marriage any more, and I don't know what to do!"

She expected to feel embarrassed afterwards, or at least self-conscious, but she did not. Something had been released, and she felt quite calm. But the calmness didn't last. The group was kind, sympathetic, helpful, even more than she had expected. They asked her if she thought her husband would be willing to go for some kind of counseling. She shook her head. They urged her to suggest it anyway, even if she knew he would say no. She didn't believe she was brave enough for that. If she had faced this much, they suggested, she would have to find the courage to face what it meant not to have much of a marriage. Did she want to try to save it, to bring it to life again? She nodded without thinking, mostly because she also did not have even the smallest amount of courage to be alone.

She drove home that night, planning what she might be able to say to him. But Richard was asleep when she got there, and she was relieved. It was enough for now just to know for the first time in a long while how she really felt about something. The rest would have to be dealt with later.

The dining room was crowded for the Intermediate meeting. Hands shot up as Paul walked in. He caught David's eye and motioned him forward. Standing in front of the group he looked at the rows of familiar faces. He would never have imagined he'd be doing something like this. "Good evening, family."

"Good evening, Dave."

From memory, stumbling only once or twice, David repeated the Center Philosophy with which every meeting was opened.

*Seeking an end to our trouble, we have, in our own ways, begun here. We discover that our pasts are left behind only when we began new lives. Alone we have failed; together we can choose to live.*

*Let us then be honest with one another.*

*Let us trust one another.*

*Let there be a feeling of concern among us, one for the other.*

*Let there be a common commitment toward personal growth and the growth of the Center family as a whole.*

*Above all, let us be unafraid to love one another.*

"Thank you, Dave," they chorused.

He was beginning to understand this philosophy now, to appreciate more and more that this was indeed, his *real* family.

He didn't know yet, although he felt it in his belly, that his other family was disintegrating.

# CHAPTER 5

LIGHTNING BUGS FLASHED, STARS WERE SHINING, AND A YELLOW light glowed in the cottage in the pines near the dark, chill lake. At the kitchen table David forked up the last mouthful of a piece of blueberry pie made from berries he and Doug had collected that morning. He listened to the chirping of the tree frogs outside the window. Every sound was clear, because nobody was talking.

It was the last night of the Petersons' vacation in Maine, planned this year to coincide with David's sixteenth birthday on August 26. He used to love to come to Lake Sebago, but this year he could hardly wait for the vacation to end.

He had been going home on weekends about once a month, taking Doug or sometimes his roommate, Eddie, along for strength. It was never easy, but he was learning to accept that it was not and probably never would be. His father had withdrawn further into silence, while his mother kept up a stream of nervous chatter. Sometimes she yelled at David, usually over something trivial, like not taking out the garbage soon enough after a meal. Then she got upset over her own anger and apologized to him. Always she cooked too much and he ate too much, because there was so little else to do. All of his old friends were negative. They called often at first, every time he came home. The network always seemed to know when he was there. But he never responded, and they soon stopped. That meant he had to spend all his time with his family, unless he and whoever came along with him could think up something to do.

David did not know how to deal with his family. It did not seem to be the same one he had left. He rarely saw his brother. Richie spent all his time with his friends when he was not working at the Burger Joint. He had finished his senior year in high school in June, and the family assumed that he would go to the community college. Then came the shock of his grades. They had been sliding during the first semester, and the second semester was a disaster. His diploma was held up until he went to summer school. Richie had said maybe he'd take a year off before making up his mind what to do. Actually he thought he had had enough of school for a while. His father was crushed. The son who had followed so dutifully in his footsteps had somehow wandered off the path. His mother said she thought if he needed some time to decide what direction to take, he should have it. The family was divided, again.

Susie regularly threw tantrums, either weeping hysterically so that everyone hated her, or locked in her room, sullen and uncommunicative. David was not sure who his sister was. She practically refused to come along on the family vacation, an annual event for as long as David could remember.

His father had always allocated one week of his vacation for the trip to Maine and used up the second week a day at a time on visits to their grandmother in Hartford, on fishing trips, and sometimes on projects around the house. His mother had tried once or twice to suggest that the two of them ought to go away somewhere without the children, but they had never done that. She had also asked that they go to a place that was more of a vacation for her, where she did not have to do all the cooking and cleaning as though she were still at home but without any of the conveniences. But nothing had changed. They went back to Lake Sebago each year, to the same cottage with the same grease-caked stove and rust-stained bathtub that had to be scrubbed when they got there and again before they left.

Kevin had advised David to take somebody along with him on the Maine vacation. It sounded like a rough time coming up. He invited Doug Mitchell, even though he knew Doug's table manners still set his mother's teeth on edge.

The boys spent their time fooling with an old rowboat on the beach and going for hikes around the lake. Susie met some kids staying in a cottage down the road and hung out with them constantly, seldom even bothering to come back for meals, except for the night of David's birthday when they all went out for lobster. They insisted, though, that she be with them on the last night before they returned home. Wanting to spend her last night at the lake with her friends, she was more petulant than ever.

The meal passed in almost complete silence. Nobody, including Richie, seemed to have anything to say. Then, as he was bunching up the last crumbs of the pie, David saw the silent tears running down his mother's face and splashing onto the table. She didn't try to stop them or even to wipe them away. David opened his mouth to say something and then closed it again. His father stared at her and finally placed his fork on his empty plate. He cleared his throat and they all waited for whatever was coming.

"This will be our last vacation together," Richard Peterson announced in an angry, husky voice, his eyes on her but his words addressed to the rest of them. "Your mother and I are planning to get a divorce."

David looked at him and then at his mother; the tears appeared to be flowing out of marble statue, and Richard's face was impassive. David didn't seem to be able to move to speak, or even to think. After a long silence his father said, "Things . . . have not been going well for us for a long time. We believe it will be better for everybody if we separate as soon as I can find a place to live."

"Is there any more pie?"

David could not believe that he had actually said such a stupid thing, but the words were out of his mouth. Neither could he believe what he had just heard, although on some level he felt the truth of it. He had known that things were getting worse, but he had never allowed himself to think it could be so bad that they'd actually get a divorce. And at this awful moment of understanding, he asked for another piece of pie.

His father reared back, glaring at him, but his mother moved mechanically to the counter and cut him another slice. "Would anyone else care for more?" Her voice sounded like a nail going through a piece of splintered wood. Richie passed his plate in silence.

"Me," said Susie, her face a perfect mask.

And not another word was said about the divorce.

That night Doug's whisper floated up from the bottom bunk. "Did you know this was going to happen?"

"I don't know if I did or not."

He had trouble falling asleep, his mind running over the same questions. What was it going to be like now? He was frightened without knowing what he was afraid of. He wondered if he was the reason for the breakup. Certainly he had caused a lot of disagreement between them. But the black sheep of the family, the scapegoat, seemed to be doing better now than either Richie or Susie. Maybe that was what was making his father leave. All these changes. David was glad he was going back to the Center and not to the house on Gilmore Street.

But everything was tense at the Center, too, a feeling of threads twisted so tight you knew something was going to snap but you didn't know what or when. On Thursday afternoon word filtered down from Paul Kendricks that all Labor Day weekend leaves were cancelled and a special house meeting had been called for that evening, everybody present, no exceptions. The housekeeping crew was instructed to take all the available folding chairs down to the basement right after dinner and get them set up. Everyone must be ready to start at six o'clock.

To start *what*? They ruminated at supper on the possibilities; maybe it was a General Meeting, one of those terrible sessions when someone who had broken one of the cardinal rules had to stand up in front of the family and be confronted by the whole group. Maybe they were going to announce some job changes. But David agreed with the older members who guessed it was probably going to be a guilt session. Knowing only heightened the tension. David wondered how he would react and what he would let go.

They knew their guess was right when all the high rollers marched in with somber expressions. First Dr. Stone, the psychiatrist, a good guy whom all the kids liked. David talked with him every couple of weeks. Next, George Miller, the psychologist and the sharpest dresser at the Center, always at the big meetings. Wayne Hollander, a tough guy like Paul Kendricks, who worked with him; nobody messed around with those two. Phil, in charge of getting people admitted, plus the supervisors who kept track of those in each phase of the program. And the eight counselors who were on duty that evening. They spread themselves around the room. David checked to see where Kevin was; he spotted him leaning against the rear wall near Betsy. In a way David was sorry Betsy hadn't stayed on as his Intermediate primary counselor. She was much tougher than he expected her to be. She didn't have the hot temper that Kevin sometimes unleashed, but she could be so even and controlled that it was almost as bad.

Paul Kendricks launched the guilt session with an explanation for those who had not been through one before. They held them a couple of times a year when staff got the feeling there were people at the Center who were carrying a lot of guilt. Sometimes the guilt was an old matter, something that had been hanging over them for a long, long time, and the longer it went the harder it got to cop to it. Maybe, he suggested, they tried to tell themselves they'd forgotten about it, that it was a small thing and didn't amount to very much; hardly worth mentioning.

"But it *is* worth mentioning. Keeping it in is not being honest. There is no such thing as *degrees* of honesty. You're either totally honest or you're not. And if you're not being honest, you're not changing. There is no such thing as 'forgetting,' even though you may tell yourself you have. Every time somebody mentions whatever it is you've done, your belly flips. I'll bet there isn't a single belly here right now that isn't flipping about something you've been holding back. So let's get started. Let's cop to some of this guilt you're holding. Get it out, clean it up. Now who's going to start?"

For a moment no one stirred. David glanced around out of the corner of his eye. He could almost taste the tension, like metal, in his mouth. Nobody said anything, so the other high rollers started piling it on, repeating what Paul had said in their own words. *Guilt.* Everyone in this room was holding some kind of guilt. Now was the time to get it out, get rid of it, start clean.

David turned around, startled at the sound of a girl's voice behind him. Sharon was one of the new members. She hadn't been in the program more than three weeks, but she nervously admitted to stealing fifty cents from her roommate's piggy bank.

"Tell us about it, Sharon," Yvonne urged.

Stammering badly, she described how she had slipped open the bank and taken two quarters to pay back a loan from another girl. Somehow she got through the confession and the explanation. Paul wasn't particularly hard on her, but he pointed out to her how stupid it was for her to do it. And George held her up as an example to the others. "If this girl who has been in the program less than a month can stand up and say this, how about the rest of you?"

Slowly they began to open up. Soon everyone in the room was raising a hand. Their guilt ranged from minor matters to serious offenses, but all involved a question of honesty. A boy admitted to gambling. A girl confessed that she had eyes for another girl in the program and for her counselor, Betsy. Several had been driving their parents' cars without licenses. A boy said he cheated on some tests at school. Another boy talked about suicidal feelings that often made him drive too fast.

Staff had decided not to make this an amnesty session, as they had sometimes done in the past, because some people tended to hoard their guilt until an amnesty was declared. But getting high was grounds for being kicked out of the Center, so they did make the situation easier: if you had been getting high, and admitted it now, you would not be thrown out, and you would not have to go through a general meeting. But you would have to go through a learning experience—a hookup—and probably get a haircut. Two people admited getting high a few months ago. Another confessed that he had been drinking at home on weekends. Others stood up to say they had stashes at home, of marijuana or of the papers or the pipes. Why had they held out so long? they were asked. Some of them were well into Intermediates and had had the stashes since before they came into the program. "Forgot," they said.

"Bullshit," Paul said.

When the confessions seemed too trivial, staff sensed that people were throwing out "bones" and withholding the real meat. But from most come deep admissions of guilt. Sex was at the bottom of many confessions: having eyes for other people, trying to set up situations that could lead to sexual encounters, becoming obsessed with masturbating.

The pressure built within David to say what he had to say and get it over with. When Paul called his name he stood at his place, nervously shuffling his feet and chewing on a wad of gum that had lost all flavor and elasticity. His voice was so low that they asked him to repeat the few words he had already said and to speak up. He recalled from months ago having eyes for Carla, trying to look down her blouse to see her breasts, and then denying that he had done it. Sometimes he still did have eyes for her, but it was not so bad now. He stood among them, sweating with embarrassment.

"We keep telling you over and over, it's normal to have these sexual feelings. It's important that you get them all out and talk about them, learn how to handle them." Paul was speaking to all of them, but then he turned to David. "Where you keep fucking up, Dave, is that you *lie* about it when somebody confronts you. You've been in the program a year, and you still haven't learned to be honest!"

The room was hot and stuffy. Time went by. Staff kept the pressure on, and just when it seemed they had squeezed everyone dry of the last drop of guilt, someone else copped to something. The session lasted for several hours. When it finally ended, the day-care people went home with their parents who had come to pick them up and the residents dragged themselves wearily off to bed. Everyone was exhausted but in an odd way refreshed, too. ". . . a lot to deal with in groups," David heard Paul say at the end. So that was what they'd be doing over Labor Day.

Lying in his bed, David thought back over the session. When he had first come into the Center, he could not understand how the counselors and the older program members always seemed to know when somebody was lying or holding a load of guilt. He had sat through groups in which somebody got killed by the other members, and it had seemed to David that the kid must really be telling the truth. But the others would say, "No, he's lying. I know he's lying." It could go on for weeks like that. And it would turn out they were always right in the end. After a while David had learned how to spot it when somebody was eaten up by guilt, and he knew how it had to go: You either copped to it or you split. You couldn't hold it and get all the way through the program.

Starting regular public high school in September turned out to be much harder than David expected. His months of tutoring at the Center School had brought him up to grade level or close to it in his major subjects, but the change from small classes—sometimes only two or three students and never more than six—to the big, impersonal classes of a large suburban school was a shock. The local high school had special education programs to help students from the Center get back into the mainstream. David's math was fine and he was assigned to a regular eleventh grade algebra class, but his language skills were still shaky; the reading problems had improved, but not enough.

When he first heard that the special education department administered the relatively small classes into which he was assigned, David balked. Special ed in his mind represented retarded kids, or maybe deaf children. Then Mrs. Aldrich, the director of education at the Center, set him straight. "Everybody learns differently, okay? At different rates and in different ways. Some people talk about learning disabilities, but I don't like that term. Call them learning differences. In order to be mainstreamed in the regular classes, you're going to have to overcome some of the differences that make it hard for you to move along with most of the other students. But please get this through your thick skull: nobody thinks you're retarded, and that's definitely not what special education means. There's a program for the gifted in the same department, so you're traveling in first class company."

But still it wasn't easy and not just because the classes were so difficult. He felt alienated. Jim Dahl drove him to the high school each morning and picked him up each afternoon. During the day he sometimes saw people from the Center, but they were far outnumbered by the others, most of whom were negative. David had never realized quite how many people got stoned. It seemed as though they nearly all did. He began to understand what was going to happen when he phased out and spent most of his time away from the Center. Where was he going to find any friends?

Kevin was trying to get him to find some girls he could talk to and eventually date. He discovered that he had not the faintest idea of how to talk to a girl or what to talk about. In groups they confronted him for not making friends with girls at the Center, for avoiding them because he was afraid he'd get eyes for them. To show them he was trying, he told them about the tall red-headed girl in his math class. But he didn't tell them that each time he had tried to start a conversation with her his throat had gone dry and his mind had gone blank. She looked at him with a half-smile and turned away to talk to her friends, people with minds full of things to say and voices strong enough to say them.

And as if that weren't bad enough, going home for weekends continued to be a dreaded chore. Mostly he tried to avoid it, but Kevin insisted he had to learn to accept the situation. His father was still living in the house, sleeping in the family room. His mother cooked for everybody and they all filled their plates and then went somewhere by themselves to eat. Nobody sat down for a meal together. Richie rarely came home at all anymore. Susie ran around until all hours. Without consulting each other, his parents alternately let her get away with whatever she

wanted to do or came down on her hard, insisting that she practically sign in and out. David had given up trying to talk to any
of them.

Slowly he slid into a depression from which he did not
know how to pull himself. At one time he had related fairly
well in groups, but no longer. He seemed stunned, almost like a
sleepwalker. Kevin kept after him: "Let yourself be more open to
your friends here, let them know how you feel, how much it
hurts. Then do whatever you can on the outside to meet new
people and to find some way of getting along with your parents."

And then the bottom fell out of David's world completely.
Doug split.

He refused to believe it when they told him. Not Doug.
Anybody but Doug, his closest friend, the person he loved most
since Jay had graduated in June. He demanded explanations:
*why?* "He must have had a whole belly full of guilt, Dave. That's
the only reason." Kevin tried to comfort him. "Everybody gets
burned a few times around here, Dave. But that doesn't mean
you stop trying."

How could he not have noticed that something was wrong?
Slowly he began to realize that all the time he had been dwelling
on his own misery, Doug had been slipping away. That made
it at least partly his fault, David thought; he had to find Doug
and talk to him. Paul Kendricks said they had gotten in touch
with his mother. She had told them Doug was home, but she was
trying to convince him to go back to the Center. Why had he
gone home? David knew he didn't get along with his family,
especially that stepfather. David was positive he could make
Doug come back. But he also was positive staff wouldn't let him
try. Once someone had split, even his best friends weren't allowed to speak to him.

For a week he worried and fretted, and one day at school he
couldn't take it any longer, walked out of the cafeteria at lunch-

time, and did not report for his next class. He went to look for Doug.

It wasn't hard to find him. He simply asked around at a few of the old hangouts at the west end of town where Doug lived. They, at least, hadn't changed. Maybe everything else was different, but kids were still hanging out at the same old places. Everybody had seen Doug, and within a few hours David had found him.

He looked bad. He had been stoned almost the whole time since he split, and he had had a couple of beers already that afternoon. "I just couldn't take it any more, Dave," he said blearily.

"Why not?" David demanded in tears. "Why in hell *not?*"

"I dunno. Too many rules, too much of everything. I just kept thinking about how nice it was when I used to get high. You know? I mean, if the choice is whether I want to live a long straight life or a short happy one, I guess I'll cut a few years off the other end."

"Listen, you got to come back."

"No, not me. But you should. You're doing good there. C'mon, though, let's just smoke this joint for old time's sake. Don't you want to, Dave?"

One toke and he'd split too. He would never be able to face them. And yet here was his best friend, one of the two people he loved most in the world. Doug rolled the joint, lit it, inhaled deeply, and passed it to David. David held it, weighing the tiny thing balanced between his fingers and what it meant. Then he dragged on it and passed it to Doug, and before long the old familiar feeling rolled over him and he relaxed. He felt good again. Nothing mattered. The Center, his family, school, the whole shitty world seemed pleasantly far away. The only thing close and important was Doug.

After a long while it was time to go—somewhere—but David didn't know where. Doug said he couldn't come home with him, because things were really strung out at his house. His mother was furious that he had split, and his stepfather was threatening to have him arrested. David couldn't stand the thought of going to his own home. He didn't want to be with his parents under any circumstances, and certainly not under these.

For a few hours he walked the streets alone. He had only a couple of dollars and no ideas. Somehow, now, he was glad to get away from Doug. Something had happened to Doug, but he couldn't quite pin down what it was. Doug had betrayed him by leaving the Center, and now David was betraying his other friends. He kept walking, getting tired, hungry, cold, scared. At last he fished in his pocket and found a dime. Then he looked for a phone booth and called the Center. It was beginning to get dark. He asked for Paul Kendricks; he knew he'd have to face him anyway, so he might as well start there.

"It's Dave. I'm coming back," he said and hung up. He had just enough money for a hamburger and a soda, and he ate standing up in the glare of neon lights. And then he started the long walk back to the Center, dread of what was coming surging in him like nausea.

Betsy had the wake-up shift and was about to leave for the day when the word came in that David had apparently left school at lunchtime and had not returned. She had promised herself from the outset that she was not going to get upset when one of the kids split. It was an occupational hazard. She kept telling the kids in her groups: you'll get hurt often, get used to it, you can't let it get to you, take another chance. But when they told her David Peterson had split, she cried, even though she was not his primary counselor any more. The tears surprised her. It had been a long time since she had done any crying, really not since she had broken her engagement. At the time grief had almost overwhelmed her. Now the tears felt good.

These days she had a hard time remembering the man she'd planned to marry. Lately her mind had been a lot on Kevin Murphy, and that surprised her, too, almost as much as her rush of tears. While she valued his friendship and felt very warmly toward him, she knew he wanted more than simple friendship, and she wasn't at all sure she had anything to offer him. She had plenty of men friends, enjoyed her freedom and her independence, and had no desire to jump into a relationship with anybody—especially not somebody from the Center, with all the problems that would entail. She would have to stop thinking about him. Put him out of her mind.

That evening at home she was listening to Bach, her favorite tranquilizer, when the phone rang. It was Kevin. "Dave is back."

"Those kids are so *dumb*," she said, tearful again, this time with relief. "It takes them so long to learn anything."

"Yeah, but when they *do* learn, they're absolutely beautiful."

Telling her about David was just Kevin's excuse for calling her. When they had gone into the city to see various photography exhibits last winter, Betsy had made it clear that she was not ready to begin a serious relationship that would create problems for both of them at the Center. So he waited and went out to New Jersey occasionally and sometimes dated a girl from his psychology class. But lately he sensed a change in Betsy. "Let's have dinner this week," he said.

She hesitated and then accepted. Surely there was nothing wrong with two coworkers from the Center sitting down and having a meal in a restaurant instead of the Center dining room. But was she being completely honest with herself? She would think about it later. The Bach concerto came to an end and Betsy climbed into bed feeling relaxed and happy. David was back. That must be the reason.

David had seen many others go through it, so he knew what to expect. But knowing it in his head was nothing like experiencing it. Paul, Wayne, and a couple of others really blew him away when he stumbled into the staff office, his knees weak and trembling and his mouth too dry to work. He told them where he had gone and why and what he had done. He told them everything, even about getting high. There was no point in hiding anything now.

"You stupid asshole!" They tore into him. "You dumb shithead! What ever possessed you to do such an idiotic thing! And now you want to come back. B-i-i-g deal! Well, you've been here long enough to know what that means. You're going to have to convince the family to take you back. And after what you've pulled, you're going to have to do one hell of a convincing job. Do you have the guts to go through with what you'll have to go through to be a part of the family again?"

He hoped to God he did.

They put him on the chair, a hard metal folding seat in a corner of the dining room facing a large sign taped at eye level: DON'T BLOW THIS CHANCE. He had stenciled the sign himself a few months ago when he was on the communo crew. He had to ask permission to go to the bathroom and have someone accompany him and wait for him while he went. They brought him a tray of food after everyone else had eaten and the cleanup crew was working on the dining room. It seemed to David that they loaded his plate with food he especially disliked and scrimped on the good stuff. It didn't much matter. His stomach churned; he didn't really want the food. What he wanted was a cigarette, but that was denied. He wondered how long they'd keep him on the chair. It varied with the offense and the attitude of the person. He was sick of it, the chair was cold and uncomfortable, and his butt ached.

"Straighten up, Peterson."

A creepy OR, pulling him up. The punky kid had heard some of the older members do it. Nevertheless, he straightened.

He had a lot to think about. He despised himself. He had really blown it. Everything in his life was going wrong. His parents had broken up; there was no family any more. One of his two best friends had split. The pain of Doug's departure was still with him, a betrayal. Who could he trust? Now he couldn't even trust himself, because he had done this stupid thing. He couldn't believe he had been so moronic. He knew when they had the General Meeting for him they wouldn't go easy. He had certainly been at the Center long enough to know better, to understand that this was what happened: you reached out to people, you let them get to know you, you let them get close, and sometimes you got burned. That was just the way it was. You had to take that risk. And you didn't go haywire when you got burned. You just took a deep breath and tried again. You didn't split or go out and get high. You didn't ever let it get to you that way. You had to find your own strength. He had thought he was stronger. It seemed not.

He thought about his year in the program. Remembering how in the begining he had said over and over, making a pact with himself, "I won't stay." Remembering the people like Jay who had pulled him through those first days when he was so miserable, those first weeks when everything was so new and strange and the pressure had seemed unbearable. A rule for everything, and they were on you immediately if you ever broke one. Slowly, slowly you learned the rules, and you accepted them. There was nothing else to do. They never let you get away with anything. Not just staff but the other program members, too.

There was always somebody around to pull you up if you slipped on even the slightest thing. It made you mad at first, and frustrated, and you thought you couldn't take it, especially if you were used to ignoring rules, or deliberately breaking them, or making up your own as you went along. At first you played along with their rules just to stay out of trouble. It wasn't worth the hassle. Once in a while, of course, you'd try to see what you could get away with. And one of two things happened: either you got caught, because everybody seemed to be watching out for everybody else. Or you didn't get caught by somebody else but by your own feelings of guilt.

He had never thought much about honesty before he came to the Center. Being honest used to mean telling the truth when you figured a lie would get you into more trouble. But now the definition had changed. For the past year he had been preached to, and had preached to others, about the need for total honesty —never to hedge or try to slide away from the truth. Not only to other people but to yourself. It was a hard thing to learn when you were used to being sneaky. It meant being honest about your feelings, too. Learning to say that you hurt, if you did, to admit that you felt lonely, if you were. Learning to be open instead of closed.

If he had been honest, he knew now, he would have told somebody right away how bad he felt when Doug left. He wouldn't have carried that pain around secretly, and then he wouldn't have done the stupid things he had done.

Now it was all down the tube. He was starting at zero again. He had just been made kitchen ramrod, a job he had really wanted. Being in charge of the kitchen crew carried a lot of responsibility. If he made it through the General Meeting, he'd be stripped of his job function and hooked up again. Weeks of sweating it out, either in the dishpan or on bathrooms or washing down the walls. He'd hate it. But he couldn't look that far ahead.

He had to get through the General Meeting first. Kevin came to tell him it was going to be that afternoon, his third day on the chair.

The furniture in the staff office looked as though it had been attacked by vandals, but it was merely worn out and money to replace it did not exist. The shag rug of an indeterminate color was matted and the loops were starting to unravel. The sofa sagged, its plastic upholstery was cracked, peeled, and in some places worn away entirely. The beautiful old fireplace had been blocked off, the ornate marble mantle obscured, the walls covered over with notices. For some reason a wristwatch, minus its strap, had been suspended from a nail high up on the wall, and the staff meeting before David's General Meeting opened with considerable speculation as to whether there was a giant cuckoo concealed in the wall behind it.

When they were done with the clock discussion, George Miller announced that a new kid had just been admitted to the Center. The boy looked about twelve, all pink cheeks and wide eyes, but he was really fifteen and had a history of sexual acting-out. "That is to say, friends, he has a thing about exposing himself to little girls."

One of the OR boys with a reputation for having a terrible temper had so far not slugged anybody, but he had used the threat of his uncontrollable anger to manipulate people. Paul advised them not to take chances with Sammy. "Don't blow this kid away unless you've got somebody around to pick you up after he knocks you on your ass. He could be dynamite, but we don't know yet."

Mrs. Cahill reported that a girl who had split a month ago and then come back thought she might have gotten pregnant. Rosalie Pecorini was going to have her tonsils out and she was scared to death. Betsy was going to take her to the hospital since her parents weren't around, but in the meantime the kid needed a lot of support.

And David Peterson was scheduled for his General Meeting. "Don't go easy on this kid," Paul said. "He's been acting like Mr. Positive for too long, and I think he's been getting away with murder. We've been playing it too soft. He needs a lot of pressure right now if he's going to make it. And while we're at it, let's get on that other goof, Peter Barlow. I have a feeling something's up with him, because he's been coming off to just about everybody around here."

"Vanessa Hoffman, too," Byron Hopkins added. "Might as well make it a learning experience for her, too."

Their approach worked out, they called in an expediter and told him to get everyone into the dining room. Another expediter got David off the chair and brought him to the staff office. He looked thoroughly terrified. "You've seen these before," Paul told him harshly. "You know what's expected of you. If you want to come back into this family, you'd better make it good."

While everyone assembled in the dining room, David waited on the landing of the elegantly curving stairway in the lobby. He stood with his feet planted far apart to keep from losing his balance, clenching his hands together to stop the trembling. *Oh God, let this be over soon. . . .* His stomach was knotted, and when he sucked in deep breaths, he felt dizzy. What if he was going to be sick? At the thought of throwing up in front of everybody, he gagged. But he swallowed hard, and at that moment Kevin opened the dining room door at the foot of the stairway and motioned to him.

"Come down now, Dave."

He tried to read the expression on Kevin's face. His hands and feet felt large, and a nerve twitched in his cheek.

He stood in front of the family that stared at him silently from the rows of seats. A couple of staff members were standing in the back of the room, arms folded over their chests. They didn't look friendly; they didn't look angry; they didn't look as though they even recognized him. He listened to the ringing in his ears. Everyone waited.

"All right, now why don't you tell us where you've been and what you've been up to, Dave."

He swallowed and worked his jaw. "I was upset because Doug left and so a few days ago I went to find him. . . ."

"Louder!"

"I said I was upset," and he repeated what he just said, his voice sounding metallic in his ears, as though it were coming through a long tube. He told them about going to look for Doug and then about going to the Super Kool. They wouldn't let him leave out a single detail, and they kept reminding him to speak up. He could feel the sweat start to trickle down his back.

"Dave!" someone called out to him. "Hey, Peterson, how come you acted like such an asshole?"

And then everybody started yelling at once, Paul's voice rising hard above the clamor. "They want reasons, Dave. They want explanations! And you better start giving it to them!"

He tried. He tried to grab the words that were stuck somewhere behind his mind. The yelling went on and on, and he tried and tried to focus on what they were after, what they wanted from him, the reasons.

"But how does it *feel* to be such a fuckin' creep?" they demanded. "How does it *feel* to betray all the people here who have been so good to you for such a long time? How does it *feel*, Dave?"

*Feel . . . feel . . . feel.* "It feels low," he shouted back to them. Something inside him started to give way, to cave in, to crumble, and the tears began. He heard their shouts, heard his own sobs, felt the tears surge up mixed with hurt and shame, and it all poured out together. He lost all sense of time, of space, even of the weight of his own body. The kept on yelling and he knew it wasn't going to stop. He squeezed his eyes shut and saw only the redness and blackness of the inside of his mind.

"Look up!" Paul ordered. "Open your eyes and look at these people! They want some answers from you. They want to know what it is you want from them."

Suddenly the room dropped into stillness and quiet. David heard his voice, very soft, say, "I need your help. I really do."

Paul's voice was softer, too. "If you need their help, then ask for it."

"I need your help," he repeated.

"If you want help, *ask* for it, stupid! Let's hear it!"

"I need your help!"

"Louder!"

"I need your help! I need your help!"

"You got to do better than that."

He was nothing any more, nothing but a voice screaming out his need. He did need them, his heart pounded, his voice echoed in his head, he thought he would surely fall down if they didn't catch him now, give him the strength he had to have, he couldn't make it without them. "I need your help!" *Oh God, they've got to help me, everything else is shit, everything, only here, only with them. . . .* "I need your help!"

"Keep it up, Dave! Keep it up! You're getting there! Let it out! Let us hear how much you need us! Do you need us bad? Then say so! Let's hear you say so!"

"I need your help!"

Their faces, straining forward, swam in front of his eyes. He thought he had seen anger and rejection in them before, but the look had changed. Then he watched Eddie stand up and move toward him. It was like a dream now, and still he was calling out to them, "I need your help!" And the tears kept on coming. "I need your help!" His voice was hoarse. Eddie floated close to him and he felt Eddie's thin, strong arms around him, holding him tight.

"You've got it, Dave," Eddie whispered to him. "You've got my help."

David hugged him back, desperately, gratefully and they held each other for a minute, rocking gently, until David's pulse slowed and the breathing came easier and his mind could perceive again where he was. Back home.

The voices were gentler now. "Sit down, Dave," Paul said, pointing to a chair. David noticed the scissors in his hand, and he sat and listened to the sound of his long hair being hacked away. He could tell by the big brown clumps dropping to the floor around him that this was not going to be a pretty cut. Everyone watched the ceremony silently. He didn't care. His hair wasn't that important to him. It was the symbol of his investment, proof that he wanted to be here enough to go through the ordeal.

"Get a broom and sweep it up," Paul ordered him curtly.

While he swept they turned their attention to Peter Barlow and then to Vanessa. Why had she come down so hard on David? What was on her mind? Embarrassed, she stood at her seat, hugging her arms. "The house flirt does not have that much mud to fling at somebody else," Paul told her. "You've been told and told. . . ."

David hardly heard them. He was weak with exhaustion, relief, release. He got the dustpan and gathered up a pile of his own rudely cut hair.

CHAPTER 6

---

"IT'S LIKE AN ESCALATOR, UP AND DOWN ALL THE TIME," DAVID
explained, pleased that he'd found the right way to express his
idea. "It's not a conveyor belt through here, that's for sure."

He was telling this between mouthfuls of baked chicken to
a woman who had come to the Center to do research for a book
she was writing. She intended to hang around for a couple of
months, she told him, to see what she could learn.

He had seen her with a supper tray, looking uneasily for a
place to sit, and had asked her to sit at his table. The other people
at the table had noticed her too and were curious about what she
was up to. She introduced herself: her name was Margaret
Snyder. When they called her Mrs. Snyder, she corrected them;
either *Ms.* Snyder or Margaret.

"*Mizzz?* Are you a women's libber?"

"Not really," she explained. "But I guess you could say I
believe in a lot of those things." They shook their heads.
Women's liberation did not flourish at the Center.

"How come you want to be called Ms.?" asked a thin boy
in a fancy embroidered shirt. "Are you divorced or something?"

She said she was. David felt his heart do a strange squeeze,
and he thought of his parents. They were getting their divorce
in a few months. His father had moved into an apartment and

133

his mother and Susie and Richie, on those rare occasions when he came home, were living in the house.

It was so bleak and unhappy he hated to go there. This year at Christmas, David had been at home. There was a pathetic little tree and his mother had tried to make a party out of trimming it. She had been crying so much Susie called her Rudolph, which made matters worse. The trip to Grandma's had been cancelled for no very good reason that David could see. On New Year's Eve his mother had gone to bed at nine o'clock, and Susie had invited a girlfriend to sleep over. David, staying up late to watch the new year come in on television, saw the two girls sneak out and dash across the snowy lawn, but by the time he got his shoes and coat on, they had disappeared. He didn't know whether to wake his mother or not. Finally he decided he would simply wait up for them. It was nearly three when they sneaked back in again. David pretended to be asleep. He had given up trying to do anything about Susie—except to worry.

Everybody at the table wanted to know about Ms. Snyder's book, and she wanted to ask them questions about the Center.

"Are you going to use real names in this?" Patty asked.

"No, I can't. Protection of privacy and all that sort of thing. And I won't even be using real people with fictional names. I'll be making up the characters, using little bits of all of you."

Nevertheless, David thought it would be neat to be a character in a book. How was she going to do this? She explained that she was just going to be around talking to people. She hoped she wouldn't make them self-conscious.

"Everybody's really open here," he assured her. "They'll tell you anything you want to know."

"Have you been in groups yet?" Patty asked.

"I will be this evening."

Ms. Snyder was in his group. When David saw there were

not enough chairs in the communo office, he brought another from the dining room for her. Ted Valentine, also known as "The Hammer," was running the group. Oh boy, David thought: this lady is really going to get an earful. All the counselors had different styles of running groups, and everybody knew Ted was the toughest and the loudest. Ted had been a counselor longer than anyone, and he supervised all the other Intermediate counselors. Nobody quite matched his style.

Ted strode in, carrying a plastic cup with his coffee, nodded to Ms. Snyder, and within about thirty seconds launched the session by confronting Pete Barlow—again.

Pete's father was a lawyer and senior partner in a prestigious law firm. David had been to Pete's house a couple of times, a huge, elaborately furnished place surrounded by acres of grass and trees in one of the expensive suburbs around Greenfield. His mother was tan and beautiful and played tennis and golf. Pete was an only child, adopted when their daughter drowned in an accident. Pete's father had been planning to send him to Harvard and to give him a place in the family firm, and this setback in his son's carefully planned life—arrest for possession of drugs, parole to the Center—had Mr. Barlow in a fury. Pete was an intellectualizer. He could *think* his way around anything. David knew this was probably the reason Pete couldn't seem to get anywhere, because he still hadn't learned to trust his feelings. Nine months at the Center, and his head and his gut were still poles apart.

David had been in group after group with him, and Pete never seemed to let go. He either remained silent and staring at his shoes or spoke in carefully articulated sentences. He had made few friends.

"Have you told anybody here that you love them?" Ted demanded.

"No."

Every person in the group was aware that Pete wouldn't make any real progress until he learned to open up. And so they kept hammering away at him—especially "The Hammer." Everybody had been putting out to him, they reminded Pete, and he gave nothing back. They probed mercilessly, looking for the vulnerable spot that would make him crack. They all knew, they all *felt*, that the only way you could change and get better was to open up and let it all pour out. Pete knew it, too—in his head.

The Hammer used sarcasm, ridicule, and any tool he could think of to break through the tough armor that often shielded a hurt and frightened human being. The kids picked up their cue from The Hammer and went after him. Pete had a knack for making everybody mad. They were all disgusted with him. The language was brutal and obscene. The volume increased. The girls, whose mouths David realized could be just as vile as the boys', were screeching.

David remembered nights when he had been in somebody else's group, in one of the other rooms down the hall, and they could hear the shouting and yelling and always knew it was The Hammer's group. It was the kind of group they both wanted and dreaded. It could pull out and get rid of a lot of pent-up, nasty, angry feelings. But if you were the one being confronted, it was a nightmare that sometimes went on for a couple of hours. And if you didn't let go then and start relating, you'd find yourself the target again and again, until you couldn't hold it in any longer.

David glanced at Ms. Snyder across from him. She sat tight and kept her eyes down. He had a moment of self-conscious embarrassment before he was drawn back into the group. "Fuck" was the operative word in all the groups, especially this one. It functioned as noun, verb, adverb, adjective, and punctuation. He hadn't realized before how it must sound to outsiders. He wondered if it bothered her, and what she thought of the whole business.

They made a bit of headway with Pete that night. In a low, halting voice he started to talk about being adopted and not knowing who his real father was. The yelling died away immediately to give Pete a chance to talk, and the voices became quietly encouraging.

"I don't know who my father is either," one of the girls said.

"Me neither," somebody added.

"Keep talking," they told him.

The father who adopted him didn't love him, Pete told them in a calm, almost monotonous voice. He believed he was not as smart as his father expected him to be, sensed he could never satisfy him, never live up to what his father wanted him to be.

"I know, I know," David murmured. That really connected. A little white flame of pain flared up. David saw his father once a week now, but they were more like strangers than ever. "Talk about your father," David urged Pete.

Little by little, it began to come out. Like picking at a knotted string, they worked on him patiently, but there was only a little reward or progress. Pete stopped suddenly and withdrew from them. Feeling cheated, the group struck out at him angrily.

"I think you've got guilt!" David said loudly, operating on the intuition they'd all developed after long experience in groups. "That's why you're afraid to open up, to tell us how you feel. That's why your head keeps playing games with you and you keep playing games with your head. Because you know if you ever start to let it out, all the guilt will come out with it."

Pete merely shook his head, and that was the end of it. They had lost him. It was like watching helplessly as a drowning person sank out of sight, unwilling even to try to swim. He had come so close this time, it seemed to David, and now he was gone. "We're not going to waste any more of this group's time on you," Ted informed him. "We're getting off your case. I can see you're relieved."

Abruptly The Hammer swung his attention to one of the girls. The house flirt had been at it again. David checked out Ms. Snyder. She was fiddling with a pendant around her neck.

He saw her around often after that and looked for chances to talk with her. She admitted that she felt very nervous when she first came to the Center. It had never occurred to David that coming here would make an adult nervous. She confessed that she had a hard time walking into a group of strangers. He felt a rush of sympathy for her. He wondered now and then about her life away from here. He wondered how she was going to write this book. They never saw her make notes or anything, but she remembered all their names. They joked with her: "Am I going to be in the book?"

"Yes," she said, "I'm using your blue eyes."

Sometimes she talked about other things she had written. They asked her if she had any children, and she told them the names of her three boys. After a while, David noticed, she started to relax and stop fiddling with her necklace so much. She told him she liked being there and felt at home.

David asked her a lot of questions about what it was like to be a writer, how she got to be one, what kind of education you had to have, and so on. It sounded like an interesting life.

He had been thinking a lot lately about his future, considering different possibilities, picking them up, examining them, laying them down again. He didn't know what he wanted to do. School was an endless struggle. His grades were above average, but he was beginning to wonder if he could handle college. It must be pretty hard. His brother Richie had given up his plans to go to community college and was more or less bumming around the country. His mother was worried and his father was mad.

He told Ms. Snyder that his parents had just gotten a divorce, and he mentioned his sister and how concerned he was about her. He'd like to ask this woman why *she* had gotten a divorce, where her former husband was, what was going on with her kids. How she felt, how they felt. Maybe she could tell him something that would help him cope with what was happening in his own family. Whenever he thought about it, he got to feeling sad and sick inside. But he didn't know if it was right to ask somebody personal questions like that. He did know that he completely dreaded going home.

Ellen Peterson was keeping a journal, started on the day she understood finally, after they came back from Maine, that her marriage was really over. When Richard had said last summer that he wanted a divorce, she had not accepted it. She did not see how she could survive it; therefore, it must not happen. She would wait, and he would eventually change his mind and they would all be happy again.

And then one morning in the fall, after he had been camping in the family room for several weeks and she had been fixing his breakfast as though nothing had changed, it came over her that she would never again have to do any of this—fry his eggs, wash his socks, empty his ashtrays. None of it. She had eaten her egg and one piece of toast and carefully put his two eggs and two pieces of toast down the disposal. When Richard had come in smelling of aftershave, she informed him that she was no longer functioning as his wife in any capacity. They had not had sex for four months, and she was not going to cook his eggs or perform any more of those wifely tasks. He had stared at her, nodded, and walked out the kitchen door. She had watched him drive away, and at that moment she had decided to begin a new life. She realized she had no choice.

She had spent the morning moving the last of his things out of the bedroom and rearranging some of the furniture to make it feel like *her* room instead of *theirs*. Then she had taken a shower, dressed, and driven to the Nurses' Registry and entered her name on the list for private duty assignments. She had driven home again and baked a large chocolate fudge cake with white icing; David was coming home the next day. In the afternoon she walked up to Gemberlings and bought a green spiral notebook in which to keep track of her new life. She had made a pot of coffee and sat down to write her first entry. And then she began to cry—again. She wondered if she would run out of tears, and eventually, for·that day, she did. But there always seemed to be more later.


David's stomach was bothering him, and he stopped by the nurse's office to talk to Mrs. Cahill. There were always people hanging around her office, claiming her attention. You could get killed in groups, pulled up on the floor, hooked up to dishpans, have your hair cut and your job position taken away, but Mrs. Cahill always had something warm and reassuring to say. David leaned on the half door and peered into her office. Her face brightened, and there came that smile.

"Well, David, what can I do for you?"

"I don't know," he complained, feeling a little better already. "I've got this stomachache, and my head hurts, and I feel sort of sick all over."

"How long have you been feeling this way?"

"All day."

"Come on in here and I'll take your temperature." It was normal. "Anything special seem to be bothering you? Everything going okay?" Even her voice was soothing.

He wished she'd let him lie down in the infirmary room next to her office, with the blinds drawn and everything quiet and far away, like when he was a little kid and he'd get sick and his mother would put him to bed and peek in every few minutes to make sure he was all right but not bothering him. He wished sometimes he could be little like that again and have her take care of him, instead of everything turning to shit the way it had when he started to grow up.

Part of his wish came true. Mrs. Cahill told him to lie down for an hour until his stomach settled down. Then he was to go lightly with the food, maybe just some soup. She was sure there was nothing seriously wrong. Probably just some minor stomach upset.

"Are you going home tomorrow?" she asked, guessing the cause of his trouble.

"Yeah."

"You'll be fine. Just watch what you eat." She patted his hand.

David really didn't know what to say to his mother on his weekends at home. It was harder since he usually went alone now. She came for him on Saturday mornings, drove him directly to the house, hovered over him in the kitchen, and watched him eat whatever she had baked for him that weekend. A couple of hours later she served a huge meal, things like roast beef or stuffed pork chops. Early in the afternoon his father would pick him up and take him to the little apartment where he had holed up with a few pieces of old garden furniture and an army cot, and they sat silently for two hours watching whatever sports program was on television. Around six o'clock they ate Kentucky Fried Chicken or pizza, and Richard drove him to his mother's home again. David had had his driver's license for over a month now, but neither his mother nor his father had let him touch the wheel.

"What did your father have to say?" his mother always asked him.

"Nothing." Which was true.

Then they settled down to watch television again. Sometimes his mother was silent, looking tired and haggard. Sometimes she talked constantly, leaping from subject to subject. She had a steady job now, taking care of a sick old lady. She was working night shift, and she wasn't used to the hours any more. She said she was thinking of selling the house and getting an apartment or maybe a smaller house in a cheaper neighborhood. Did he have any idea when he'd be moving home? When he phased out, probably. When would that be? He didn't know.

He was anxious to phase out; he thought of it constantly. But he wished he could stay at the Center instead of moving home. They had a room at the Center where Phase-Outs who didn't have a place to go could live until they graduated from the program. But he knew they'd never let him stay there. Kevin kept harping on him that he had to learn to accept what had happened. There was nothing he could do about it. It was not his fault or his responsibility, so he might as well learn to live with it. "Why don't you try to talk to your mother and father about your feelings?" Kevin asked. But he couldn't.

He curled up under the warm blanket in the infirmary and listened to the murmur of voices in the next room as other people stopped by for Mrs. Cahill's advice. She was the local expert on skin problems. Practically everybody worried about zits, and she counseled cleanliness and occasional dabs of a special cream that she must have bought by the case. Some of the kids were worried about their weight, too, especially the girls. It was easy to gain weight at the Center, because you really didn't get much exercise, just sitting around talking most of the time, and then eating got to be the big recreation. Mrs. Cahill recommended diets and passed the dieters along to Fred, the cook, for advice on what they might eat at each meal. Pimples, fat, stomachaches, minor cuts, an occasional sore throat or stuffy nose—it was an endless stream in and out, and the medicine dispensed in the largest quantity was sympathy and kindliness.

But she wouldn't allow malingering. After an hour she poked her head into the darkened room and asked David how he was doing. He wished he could say he still felt terrible so he could lie there for a while longer. But he was better, and he had to say so.

"There's some woman who's writing about the Center, did you know that?" his mother said the next day. "I met her at Parents Group last Monday."

"That's Ms. Snyder. She's okay."

It gave them something new to talk about. David wondered if his mother would start to be a Ms. after she got her divorce. He certainly hoped not.

That afternoon his father seemed tense and jittery and chewed on his pipe more nervously than ever. Finally he announced that he would have to cancel their plans to eat dinner together.

"That's okay," David said, surprised but also relieved.

Frowning, his father explained that he was having dinner with a friend. Pause, while he knocked the dottle from his pipe and tamped in fresh tobacco. The friend was a woman. Another pause while he drew the flame of a match down into the pipe bowl. "It's a lonely life," he said. "I guess I need to have somebody around."

David wondered if his mother knew why he was coming back early. He could tell that she wanted to ask, but he volunteered nothing. He decided to stay out of this. But he was curious about what kind of a woman his father had met, and where he had met her, and if there was anything going on between them. If there was, then there was less possibility that his parents would ever get back together again. He had been hoping that somehow things would work out between them. Kevin had been trying to talk him out of such unrealistic dreams.

"You still aren't accepting what *is*," Kevin observed. "You'd better try."

He was also having a hard time accepting the reality that Betsy and Kevin were going together. He had been amazed when Kevin told him around Thanksgiving, just before the two of them announced in a Morning Meeting that they had been good friends with each other for a long time and that they were now much closer and were actually going together. They would be spending most of their free time together and would probably live together to see how it would work out.

From somewhere, and quite unexpectedly, David discovered that he was jealous. He loved both of them; the fact that they probably loved each other and had a relationship that had nothing to do with him struck him as an act of disloyalty. For a while he watched them carefully, a secret spy, trying to intercept private signals between them. Although he had plenty of contact with Kevin and saw him once a week, he realized that he had not talked with Betsy for a long time. It became extremely important for him to be with Betsy, and the next time David saw her walk through the living room while they had some free time after dinner, he called out, "Hey, Betsy, want to talk?"

"Later," Betsy had said, hurrying on.

The next day he had tried again, and again Betsy was busy. She had never been so involved and preoccupied before she and Kevin got together, David was sure. Suddenly it seemed to David that Betsy was shutting him out, and it was probably because of Kevin. The next time David was in Betsy's group, he came off to her in a snotty way, without intending to. He was immediately embarrassed. He liked Betsy a whole lot, and he certainly hadn't meant to be rude. He couldn't think why he had said such a thing, but if he didn't know what was wrong, she did. She told him off, promptly and firmly. "You're jealous of Kevin, aren't you?" He didn't try to deny it.

This was the kind of thing she and Kevin talked about after that dinner date in October when they knew they wanted to be together. It was what they discussed with Dr. Stone and George Miller and the others. The first suggestion out of the mouths of the high rollers was the one they expected: one of them ought to find another job somewhere else. But neither of them wanted to leave the Center. They had given it some thought, they said, and they believed that it would be more of a loss to the Center than if they were both allowed to stay and to be together. But what if it didn't work, George Miller asked them. How would they be able to keep on doing their jobs if they broke up and had to face each other a dozen times a day? And how was this going to affect the kids? That was the main question.

Kevin argued that it would give the kids good adult role models. Every one of them was having a hard time working out a relationship with the opposite sex. They weren't allowed to get involved beyond the brother-sister stage at the Center, and they were scared to death to look for boyfriends and girlfriends on the outside. The boys were tongue-tied, unable to initiate a conversation, let alone to ask for a date. The girls clung together, trying to remember the flirtatious ways that always seemed to work the magic in love stories. They didn't trust each other. It was almost a war.

"Maybe they'll learn something about how friendship and love can grow if Betsy and I are around showing them," Kevin suggested.

"If it works," The Hammer commented. "And if it doesn't work, they'll learn how to break up miserably."

Finally, the high rollers gave their approval, but a lot of the

145

program members did not. They resented the time and attention they knew Kevin and Betsy were giving each other, and they felt cheated. Most of them, whose lives were wholly wrapped around the Center, preferred to ignore the fact that staff members had their own worlds away from there. Everybody knew that some of the staff were married and had families and that some were single and had friends. But none of that mattered very much. Having Betsy and Kevin together reminded them of those other worlds where other things, people and relationships might be more important than the Center, and that was hard to handle. For the next couple of months Betsy and Kevin had their hands full explaining their decision and their situation to their primary cases and to other kids as well.

It was Betsy's idea that she and Kevin set up a seminar on dating for the Phase-Outs and some of the older Intermediates. Nearly everybody in the program had at some point had a difficult time with sex, and it got in the way of friendship and dating. Some of the girls had been sleeping with boys from the time they reached puberty, but they hadn't the remotest idea of how to behave on a date. Most of the boys had thought of girls primarily as ways of satisfying their own needs. They didn't know how to go about getting to know girls as people.

The seminar was a good idea in theory, but in practice everything went wrong. A couple of boys in the group were dating girls on the outside, and one even had a steady girl. But the rest were a bundle of nerves and nameless fears, absolutely terrified of the prospect of even launching a conversation, and all of them weighed down with sex stereotypes that made it even harder.

It was completely up to the boys, everyone agreed, to initiate the conversation. The girl might set up a situation, might allow an opening, but she would never approach a boy and start talking to him. Betsy could hardly stand this, but there was enough to work on without trying at this moment to dispel those in-grained, old-fashioned ideas. The boys were convinced that everything was in their hands, and the girls were convinced of it, too.

Nobody seemed able to think of anything to say.

Kevin suggested that they try some role playing. After much coaxing, a boy and a girl moved their chairs to the middle of the circle and tried to improvise a conversation. They pretended they were in the high school cafeteria and that they knew each other from geometry class. She saw him pass by with his tray, and she smiled. He asked if the seat next to her was taken. She said no, but she did not invite him to sit down. He took the seat. There was a silence until he got up the gumption to ask her about geometry, saying he didn't understand the new material. She said she was having trouble, too, and was worried about passing the exam. More silence, except for the spectators who were laughing maniacally for some reason.

Betsy shushed the audience and encouraged the actors. "What next? You got the perfect opening." Finally the boy seized it: Would you like to study together some night? Yes. Tonight? Yes.

Betsy sighed and recruited David and Carla to act out the date arranged by the other two, but it seems she had hit the only two self-confident ones in the group on the first round. The rest were reduced to giggles, jokes, and general avoidance of the matter at hand. David could not think of anything to say to Carla, who gave him no help at all, and every time he caught Eddie's eye he shrugged in complete helplessness.

Giving up on the role playing idea, Kevin and Betsy tried to explain how they conducted their courtship, how they got to know each other at the Center, how it was a whole lot easier when you met somebody you had something basic in common with, like a job, and how that gave them a lot to talk about in the beginning. Then they discovered they were both interested in photography, and that added another dimension. Of course, they admitted, there was a strong physical attraction, but that was something that had to be put aside until some other things had been worked out in their relationship.

After it was over Betsy and Kevin went out for a beer together to recover. "Do you think anything we said made a dent in their thick preconceptions?" Betsy wondered.

"Maybe a few. Peterson's ears were glowing, and that's usually a sign of something going on in his head."

Nothing seemed to stand still in one place long enough for David to learn to deal with it, and he often felt depressed without knowing exactly why. Outwardly things seemed to be going well. He had been made an expediter, and he wore a necktie and good pants, and the expediter's notebook stuck out of his hip pocket. He was very busy with his duties, and he had trouble finding time to keep up with other things, like homework. Expediting took a lot of energy; he was very tired.

He was often accused in groups of stuffing his feelings and not coming out with what was bothering him. They never let him forget that he had been in the program for sixteen months, his name was pretty close to the top of the Intermediate pop-sheet—the list of people in that phase of the program, according to the length of time they've been there—and some people lower on the list than he were likely to be phasing out soon. He wanted badly to make Phase-Outs, and he was still jealous of people who were doing better than he was. School was still a struggle, and he had not yet made any friends there. He wished he had a girl, but he was absolutely unable to get up enough nerve to talk to any in his classes. His visits home were dismal. His mother talked about being lonely and worried about money and tried to look brave when she told him she had put the house up for sale. He didn't know what he wanted to do with his life. He heard through the grapevine that Doug had been picked up for dealing in drugs. Nothing, nothing at all felt right.

Toward the end of January another unexplained house meeting was announced. As usual, an air of anxiety permeated the atmosphere, and at supper, as usual, everybody speculated on what this one might be about. Once again all the chairs were set up in the basement; David grabbed a seat near his friends, and everyone was ready and on edge by six o'clock. He saw Ms. Snyder sitting in the back; she nodded and waved to him. When the staff filed in promptly at six, David noted with relief that they were relaxed and smiling. He whispered to Eddie, "It can't be anything bad. They all look pretty pleasant."

"What we're here for tonight," Dr. Stone said, without wasting any time, "is to announce the new Phase-Outs and some job changes." David's heart was thumping so furiously it made his shirt flutter, and his breath ran fast and shallow. God, how he wanted to hear his name on that list!

Betsy made the first announcement: "This person has been in the program for a long time, and he's gone through a lot of changes and grown quite a bit. There have been plenty of times when I didn't know if he'd make it, but he has at last. Eddie Simmons." Next to David, Eddie leaped to his feet with a jubilant shout. David jumped up and hugged him, thumping him on the back; other friends threw their arms around him. Then Eddie broke loose and lunged to the front of the room, where he nearly knocked Betsy over with an enthusiastic embrace.

Ted "The Hammer" made the next announcement, and another of David's friends was boosted out of Intermediates and into the ranks of Phase-Out. The list went on, the tension growing among those who hoped to hear their names. And then it was over, and ten people David knew well were Phase-Outs, and he was still an Intermediate. He fought down the disappointment that welled up and threatened to choke him.

Paul Kendricks was talking. "Probably there are some of you who are disappointed, but I think you all knew if you were going to make it when we first started reading the list. If you were asking yourself the question, 'Will I?', then you probably already knew the answer. Is there anybody here who really expected to make it but didn't?"

Tentatively David raised his hand. He didn't know if he was being entirely honest or not. There had been times when he was quite sure he would phase out, but there had been those other problems that sometimes seemed to be dragging him back. Carla's hand was raised, too. The same disappointment he was feeling was etched clearly on her face, and she was trying hard not to cry.

Paul and a couple of others exchanged knowing smiles. "It's kind of a coincidence that you both feel that way. Because we're going to announce some job changes now, and it seems that our two new shingles are David Peterson and Carla MacLoughlin."

Shingle! In charge of all the male expediters! It might not be as good as phasing out, but it was a tremendously demanding job. David swallowed hard, torn between conflicting emotions: the letdown of not phasing out, the elation that he had been chosen for such a responsible position, and the question of whether he would be able to handle the job. They obviously believed he could. A little dazed, he stood up to receive the good wishes of his friends, who hugged and pounded him. He hugged Carla, who would now be over all the female expediters. They were good friends now; he had finally managed to get over having eyes for her, either quickly suppressing forbidden thoughts about her or getting out of her way when they surfaced.

The announcements were still going on. New expediters.

New ramrods for all the crews. Some of the ORs were assigned to crews for the first time. Everybody seemed happy. Amazing, David thought. He could remember sixteen months ago when he had promised himself that he absolutely would not stay. And here he was, with one of the two most important jobs in the house. Ms. Snyder came up to him after the meeting to shake his hand and wish him good luck. He made up his mind to spend as much time as he could with her, teaching her about the Center. He wanted her to write a good book about the place that would tell people what it was really like here.

Most people, he had discovered, didn't know anything at all about the Center or had all sorts of misconceptions about it. A lot of people still thought it was for heroin addicts, the way it had started out originally. They didn't realize that it had changed. At school people were always bad-rapping the place. Some of the kids—and some adults, too—believed it was just a place where you got brainwashed to mouth a lot of stuff about the evils of drugs. Most people didn't understand that the Center was a place where you *changed*—not just stayed straight. That was only part of it. Some people thought it was a nuthouse of some kind. He found himself doing a lot of explaining, saying the same things over and over. Sometimes he got tired of it.

"Listen," one boy had said to him. "What's so bad about grass? I can see that maybe heroin is a bad thing, and maybe acid and coke and glue and speed and all the rest of that. A lot of guys don't believe all the shit about bad-tripping and so on. It gives you a high or a hallucination, or whatever, so they do it. I've read all the propaganda about that stuff, and I can sort of see the point. But what's so bad about smoking pot? It isn't addictive. You don't get a hangover. It doesn't rot your liver or kill your brain cells. It seems to me it's a hell of a lot safer than alcohol, which is just a legal drug anyway. And nobody has come up with any *positive* proof that pot does any kind of damage to your brain or your chromosomes or anything. So what do you guys think is so bad about getting a nice mellow feeling from a reefer?"

It was the standard argument. He had heard it a million times. Patiently David ran through his answer. "Maybe for some people there's nothing wrong with smoking pot once in a while. But, man, I was getting high all the time. I couldn't even go through a day without getting stoned. Being stoned was more important to me than everything else, than *anything* else. It was the only reality, you know? Then I started getting into all kinds of trouble, doing lousy in school and all. Maybe it isn't that way for everybody, but it was for me and for all of us at the Center. Maybe now that I know a lot more about myself I could handle it, just get high once in a while without letting it take over my life. But I'm not going to run the chance."

When the kids at school asked him if he ever thought about getting high, he admitted that he did—that he used to think about it all the time, but now just once in a while he forgot about the shitty part of feeling lonely and all and just remembered that nice feeling of having everything kind of fade away.

"Aren't you tempted to try it again and just *see* what it's like now?" they pressed him.

"Yes, but I won't do it."

"Once can't hurt, and anyway, who would know?"

"I would."

Then he walked away. He had had lots of conversations like that.

"What are your plans for the future, Davey?"

He had brought his report card along to show his father, and the math grade impressed the hell out of the old man.

"I don't know yet. I'm still making up my mind."

"You don't have forever."

Which was true. He was in the second half of his junior year in high school, and pretty soon he was going to have to make some decisions about his future. He had talked to Mrs. Fitzhugh, his high school guidance counselor, and to Mrs. Aldrich at the Center. The old ambition of being a heart surgeon had faded away; it didn't seem particularly realistic since he wasn't that much of a student. Richie used to talk about being a carpenter, and now that idea appealed to David, too. Maybe he could be a builder. He was pretty good at mechanical drawing. He knew his father was hoping he'd be the one who became an accountant, but that didn't interest him at all.

For the first time, he was able to talk to his father about the future. That was safer, at least, than talking about the present or the recent past. Maybe things were changing a little between them. Not much, but a little. The distant past was safe ground, too, apparently. Chewing steadily on his pipe stem, his father told him about the dreams he had had when he was David's age. David had heard most of the story before in bits and pieces, usually as part of a lecture on laziness and ingratitude.

Richard Peterson had come from a poor family. Neither of his parents had even finished high school, but they had wanted him to go to college. They saved up enough to get him through one year; after that it was up to him. His father, a silent man, had been very strict with him. His mother had had to work extremely hard, and she wasn't very strong; she died when he was sixteen. There were several children, and he was the oldest. He had a job at a grocery store after school and saved his money—"Not like kids today," he always added pointedly. He dreamed of college, but his grades weren't good enough for a scholarship, and he was no athlete either, so he signed up for three years in the Marines. When he came out, the desire for an education had slipped away. He wanted to get a job, earn some money, find a wife, marry, settle down, have a home and a family. For a while he went to night school, still vaguely hoping to earn a degree. But the job he got demanded a lot of overtime, and that seemed more important than school. He calculated that at the rate he was going he would be about thirty when he finally finished. So he gave up. Now, at the age of forty-two, he realized that if he had kept it up he would have gotten his degree twelve years ago and maybe he'd have a job that he enjoyed.

But he said he was not sorry or bitter. He had met David's mother, Ellen Kucera, at the home of some friends. They had started dating, within two months had decided to get married, and three months after that was the wedding. It was the right person at the right time, for both of them. Richard Junior was born a year later; David two years after that. Then came Susie.

Richard shook his head sadly. He could not, he confided to David, figure out what had gone wrong. He had tried; really tried. He had honestly thought he was doing everything he should. He had worked hard, saved his money, tried to make a good home for his wife and family. He did not drink, gamble, or run around with women. He had always been faithful to his wife. He admitted he had sometimes thought about other women, but there was never anybody worth the price. So what had he done wrong?

David, surprised, saw the pain in his father's eyes. For some reason he had never considered the possibility that his strict, silent father felt anything like pain. He had always seemed so strong, so remote from the rest of them. There were a lot of questions David wanted to ask him. What about Richie? Why was Richie the favorite and not he? Susie he could understand; Susie was a girl, and the youngest. But what was there about David that his father didn't love? He wished he could ask, but he didn't know how, and he didn't know if his father would know how to answer.

"Davey, listen to me," his father said in a tone David had

not heard before. "I want you to know that I don't blame you for anything that's happened. I know I've probably done a lot of things wrong, and that a lot of the troubles you've had are my fault. I don't know what I could have or should have done differently, exactly. But I'm very pleased and happy about what you're doing. It's peculiar, isn't it, that you're probably the kid I'll be the most proud of."

David could hardly bear to look at his father's face, but when he did he saw that his eyes were glistening. He had never seen his father cry. Without stopping to think about what he was doing, he reached out and took his father's hand. It was icy cold. David's voice was hoarse when he said what he felt. "Dad . . . you know I love you."

Richard squeezed David's hand, looked at him for an instant, and looked away again. That was all there was to it. They didn't have to say anything more.

The weeks passed, some quickly, some slowly, but they went, and David raced to keep up with his hectic schedule. The van left at eight o'clock to take him to school and brought him back to the Center about two-thirty. He changed from the jeans and denim shirt he wore to school to his shingle's clothes: pressed pants, clean shirt, polka-dot tie. From then on he was on the move, supervising all the expediters under him and keeping a general eye on program members as well. Sometimes he looked with a certain envy on the ORs, who seemed to have such an easy time of it. At first they just sat around, not doing much of anything. When they got job assignments on work crews, all they had to worry about was the task in front of them. And when they got to be Intermediates and ramrods, all they had to worry about was making sure all the people on the crew did what they were supposed to. Expediting was tougher, but at least there was a bunch of expediters to spread the work around. David realized, when he stopped to think about it, that none of it was as easy as it now appeared. Pressure and responsibility were always being increased in proportion to individual ability to handle it. Still, no way in the world would David change places with an OR. Now he was at the top of the pyramid with the most status and the most responsibility; he also had the most worries.

And since he was still an Intermediate, he still had meetings and groups every Tuesday and Thursday night. Staff said he was dynamic in groups, knew how to confront somebody and make it work. He was the one who finally got Peter Barlow to open up and start talking about his resentment of his father and his own feelings of inferiority.

Occasionally he had a few hours off, but it never seemed to be enough. He wished he had more time to relax. His mother picked up on his tension when he came home on weekends. She said his foot-tapping and knee-jigging drove her crazy.

Summer came; school ended. David started looking for a job. The responsibility of an outside job was part of the process at the Center. It helped you get an idea of what you could do, where you wanted to go, and you learned something about getting along with people in the community. Most of the other guys ended up at Mister Burger or Super Kool, but by a lucky break of some kind David was hired as salad boy at a big steak house. He was in charge of the salad bar, making sure the fixings were ready, the bowls of condiments and dressing filled, the greens fresh and crisp. He enjoyed the work and took pride in keeping the salad bar always looking perfect. The guys who worked in the kitchen were stoned most of the time. That didn't bother him any more. He minded his business, they minded theirs. But the pretty waitresses all seemed to hang out with them.

On a hot Sunday night in June, everybody at the Center dressed up—the boys in suits, the girls in long dresses—for the summer graduation ceremony. David had been to several of these in the borrowed auditorium of the Catholic high school. There were the usual speeches, introductions of the staff, presentation of graduates, and as the last part of the program, the announcement of new Phase-Outs. This time David knew for sure. He heard his name, jumped up to embrace his friends, caught the look of disappointment on the faces of those who had hoped but hadn't made it.

A few days later Kevin told him it was time for him to move back home.

CHAPTER 7

THE NEW HOUSE WAS MUCH SMALLER THAN THEIR OLD ONE. There were only two tiny bedrooms: one for Susie, one for David. His mother slept in the living room on a sofa bed, the same one that used to be in their family room. The basement recreation room was gloomy and damp, but they put the rickety Ping-Pong table down there and made up an old cot to look like a studio couch, ready for when Richie came home. They hardly ever heard from him. He was still drifting around the country. "Learning about life," he said in his occasional brief notes asking for money. His mother sent him what he asked for and pleaded with him to call—collect—and let her know how he was and when he was coming home.

Leaving the old place had been hard on all of them. Ellen had cried the night she accepted the buyer's offer, but the next day she had started sorting and packing and getting ready for a tag sale. After the mortgage was paid off, half the money from the sale of the house went to Richard. David wondered what his father would do with the money. Maybe he would buy a house, too. His basement apartment seemed so dismal; all you could see were the feet of people walking by and the bottom half of garbage cans.

The house his mother had bought was only fifteen minutes from the hospital, where she now worked as a supervisor of the night shift because it paid the most. She told David she was thinking of looking for a personal life of her own, but she admitted to him that she didn't know what that would be or even where to start. The house seemed as good a place as any to begin.

She was running on raw nerves. Every room in the house had to be painted before they could move in, she decided, in addition to all the work involved in leaving the old place. David did his best to help, but they got under each other's skin. He wasn't as fast as she was, or as neat, and he certainly couldn't match her nervous energy. Still, it got finished. His new room rather pleased him, and it was nice to have a place of his own again. He had adjusted to dormitory life in the Greenhouse, but he had never gotten over the chill he felt when he had discovered over a year and a half ago that they had given his room in the old house to Susie. As soon as his father moved out, his mother had painted a coat of flat white over Susie's pink walls in the room that was now David's and had told David he could do whatever he wanted to with it from there on, but he had never bothered to do anything. After a while he had stopped noticing.

Susie's room was no longer little-girlish. No dolls and stuffed bunnies crowded the bed. Her tastes had changed to cool contemporary, and she went in for garish posters and sleek plastic. She would be fifteen in the fall. David thought she had turned out to be very pretty. She seemed to have settled down to one boyfriend, a creepy guy with a million zits who hung around much too much and always showed up at mealtime. David knew the boy got high, and he had assumed for a long time that Susie did too. He wondered if she was sleeping with Ronald. Probably. He hoped she was using some kind of birth control. Surely his mother had spoken to her about that. She was a nurse, after all, but he was not sure she was realistic about such things. Maybe he should say something. They weren't close, he and Susie, but neither were they enemies. Life was relatively peaceful in the Peterson house.

His mother worked five nights a week from eleven to seven, taking her two-day break in the middle of the week. David worked every night at the Steak Out, except the two nights he must be at the Center for Phase-Out meetings. Sometimes he drove his mother's car, a privilege he had earned by paying the large insurance premiums and filling the gas tank once a week. It was his as long as he could get home from work in time to take her to the hospital. It also meant he had to be there when she came off her shift at seven the next morning. Sometimes it was easier to hitch rides.

They had divided up the household chores. David took care of the grocery shopping, using the basic list that his mother drew up and adding whatever else he could within their tight budget. Susie did the laundry for all of them once a week. He and Susie shared the cooking, and the best times they spent to-gether were in the kitchen. He was trying to teach her what he knew, and the bread he had learned to make at the Center was now her specialty, certain to appear at least once a week.

They often argued about cleaning up. The principle was that one cooked and the other washed dishes, but David tried in vain to convince her that a good cook cleans up as he goes along, rinsing and putting things to soak. Susie managed to use every pan in the cupboard and then to leave them with the gunk drying in them. They were also supposed to keep their own rooms clean. His mother did the rest of the house. She said she didn't mind, as long as somebody else took care of the meals. He knew she would probably rather cook; she liked doing it as much as he did. What they all hated was outside work, so the yard was ragged and neglected. Richard Peterson would never have allowed that.

While they were chopping onions or peeling potatoes, David tried to get Susie to open up to him. He did not say that he couldn't stand her boyfriend. That subject was taboo. But he coaxed her to talk about things, like what she wanted to do with her life, and she came up with a different idea every time he asked her: airline stewardess, rock singer, dancer on television—nothing very realistic. He remembered how he had felt when he was her age, and he guessed she wasn't that much different than he had been, except he was a loner and she wanted an audience. She said she didn't ever want to get married, because marriages were shit. Just look what had happened to Mom and Dad!

Susie refused to spend any time with their father. She said it was all his fault that the family had broken up. If he hadn't left, they'd still have their same old house, and she'd have her same old room. David reminded her that she had changed rooms, that her "same old room" had been hers for only a year or so, and that she had never liked the one she had had before that.

She was angry at their mother, too, who, she believed, had caused her father to leave, probably because she was jealous that Susie was his pet. And then she had bought this ugly house where there wasn't any room for anything. She hated it, hated it, hated it! Susie hated her mother and she hated her father, too. She hated Richie for leaving, and he must hate all of them or he wouldn't have gone.

David tried to cut through the anger to explain that their

father hadn't left Susie and her mother hadn't made him leave because of Susie. Their parents had gotten a divorce *from each other*. He didn't really understand any more about it than she did, but he was sure it most definitely was not any one person's fault. She should stop *blaming* people, including herself.

"Besides, I haven't left," he told her. "I'm still here."

"You! All of a sudden you're so perfect, and now I'm the shit around here!" She burst into tears and flew out.

August 26: David celebrated his seventeenth birthday working at the Steak Out. When, by chance, he mentioned to the manager that it was his birthday, Mr. Farmer clapped him on the shoulder and told him to invite some friends over before they closed to eat as much as they wanted for half-price. Beer was on the house. Only two of his friends were old enough to take advantage of the free beer. Eighteen-year-olds at the Center had drinking privileges—one or two beers on an evening out—since handling liquor in moderation was one of the things they were expected to learn.

About ten o'clock that night four boys from the Center arrived in the battered car Eddie had managed to buy with his own savings. David got them a table near the kitchen and joined them while they wolfed down an average of three hamburgers apiece. Two had their allotted beers and then switched to root beer in chilled mugs. They were busy talking when the kitchen door swung open quietly and one of the waitresses carried in a birthday cake with a bunch of candles blazing on top. David was astonished, so surprised that when she set it on the table in front of him and hurried back to the kitchen, he still had not thought of a word to say.

"My God, who was that?" Eddie asked eagerly.

"I guess her name is Heather," David explained. He couldn't think of her last name or if he had even heard it.

"You *guess* her name is Heather? You mean you've got a pretty girl like that working here and you don't even know her *name?*"

They were all over him then. They had been listening to his moping complaints in Phase-Out meetings about how he never seemed to meet any girls and never got to know anybody. They had even asked him in groups, "Aren't there any girls where you work?" And he had shrugged and said he guessed there were, but he never really had a chance to get to know any of them. They were always busy and so was he. Actually he avoided them, although he didn't want to admit that. It was so much easier that way. He had known that Heather was around, but he had never tried to talk to her.

"This place is *full* of cute girls!" Pete Barlow said, waving his arms to include the cashier and a couple of waitresses who had stuck their heads out of the kitchen to watch. "What's wrong with you, Peterson? Are you blind? Or just crazy?"

"Blow out the candles, Dave, before the damned thing explodes."

He blasted them, getting all seventeen at once. The boys applauded, joined by a couple of the waitresses, who were still peering from behind the kitchen door.

"If you didn't wish for the right thing," Eddie said meaningfully, "you must be completely out of your mind."

"I did, don't worry," David reassured him.

"Then start now," Pete instructed him, "and bring some others along."

In an agony of shyness, David went out to the kitchen to look for Heather. It did seem suddenly incredible to David that she had been there all this time, for more than two months, and he hadn't tried to get to know her. A friendly person, and pretty too. Maybe a bit on the chubby side, but not too much, and her hair was so shiny he wanted to touch it. She always smiled and said hello, and although he said hello back, he had never gone any further with the conversation. Once she had even come over to him and said she thought he made the salad bar look very nice; nobody else had ever taken the trouble with it that he did. He had thanked her, embarrassed but pleased. Now that he thought about it, he realized she had made the first step. He wasn't sure that was the way it should be done, but he was glad it had happened.

When he found Heather in the kitchen, though, his tongue seemed caught in a thick web of self-consciousness, but he managed to thank her for the cake and to invite her to come into the dining room and have a slice with him and his friends. She bobbed her head and said all the girls there had pitched in on it He came back to the table with five waitresses and a grin of triumph. It turned out to be a great party after all.

Tommy Schwartz was the biggest man David had ever seen. David was a shade under six feet tall, and Tommy beat him by several inches. Furthermore, he was built like a fullback, the position he had played during his two years of college before a drug scandal caught up with him and he ended up back in his home town. He was dragged to the Center by a relative who knew somebody who had been there.

In their weekly sessions, Tommy told David a lot about his own life. Betsy hardly ever talked about herself, rarely used herself as an example of the things that could go wrong. Kevin as an OR counselor had used his personal experience as a way of pulling people in. Tommy used his to show them how to move out.

He had, he told David, probably the worst Phase-Out record on the books, which was why they had made him a Phase-Out counselor when they finally broke down and hired him. Nobody went through the program easily, but during that period when everyone else was either splitting or thinking about it, Tommy had breezed along like Mr. Positive, relating in groups, the whole business. He never had a physical haircut as an OR or an Intermediate. He got a few verbal haircuts of course, and hookups now and then, but generally he had been a model client. Very mature.

Until he had phased out, and then the real trouble began. As long as he had been totally involved at the Center, had all his friends there, his whole life there, he was fine. But when he had to go out into the community again and get a job and make friends on the outside, he couldn't handle it. Within a matter of weeks he had managed to fall in with a completely negative crowd, guys who were high all the time, hung out at bars, picked up negative girls. First thing he knew, he was right back where he had started, as though his year at the Center had never happened.

But he had copped to it and sat on the chair for a couple of days. They had made it pretty rough for him. It was, everybody agreed later, the worst General Meeting in memory. Unable to crack through that protective shell, to get in touch with the real Tommy Schwartz, they had put him back on the chair again and made him go through a second GM a few days later. That one was better. They whacked off his hair and hooked him up to washing the walls for what seemed like forever and busted him to Intermediates, back where it was safe, where he fitted in comfortably. Within a few months there didn't seem to be any reason for keeping him an Intermediate, and he made Phase-Out for the second time. Sooner or later he had to learn to handle his freedom.

A few weeks later Tommy split and stayed away for six months. During those months everything bad that could possibly happen, did. This time they didn't want to take him back. He couldn't blame them, but he knew he had to do something or his life was as good as finished. The timing was right; something had happened. He obviously no longer had a "good guy" image to protect. He couldn't fall any lower than he had. And that was when the real growth took place. When he finally graduated he tried to get them to hire him as a driver for the van, but they refused. He was still hanging too close to home. They told him to get out and make it on his own. Tommy moved to Colorado and got a job in the subscription department of a publishing company. But every week or so he would call Dr. Stone and George, hounding them for a job. Finally they relented, and he came back as a counselor the spring before David phased out.

For the first couple of months Tommy spent all his time on the floor, getting to know the people. Then he began to sit in on groups, watching to see how they were reacting. Finally they assigned him a couple of cases to get used to the paperwork and to feel his way through the first private counseling sessions. One of those cases was David.

On the second anniversary of David's arrival at the Center, Tommy called him into his office. The windows were open, and David could smell the first hint of autumn, a sort of warm dustiness in the air.

"How's it goin,' Dave?"

"Pretty good, I guess."

"You don't sound too sure about that."

David shrugged.

"Okay, let's take it one thing at a time. How's school? You're a senior now, right?"

School had just started, and David felt much better about it since he had made up his mind what he wanted to do next year. It was an idea that had popped into his head when he least expected it, although it had probably been there for a long time. Once it was settled that he wasn't going off to a four-year college, the pressure had eased. Now he dreamed about getting a job in a fancy local restaurant to learn the trade firsthand, and about maybe even opening his own restaurant some day: the kind of place where you got a regular crowd coming around because the atmosphere was relaxed and the food was outstanding and un-usual. He planned to ask his mother about some of her Czech specialties, her goulash, for instance. She could probably teach him some of what he needed to know. He had been hanging around the kitchen at the Center in his spare time—what there was of it—talking with Fred Kessler about where he had gone to school and how he got his jobs and what the possibilities were. He had always liked Fred, even when the time he spent in the kitchen had been mostly busting suds. And as Fred pointed out, Dave certainly knew more about the dirty end of kitchen work than practically anybody who went into the business.

"So what about your job?"

A couple of weeks ago David had heard about a new soup and salad restaurant that was opening in town. They were ad-vertising for a salad chef, and David thought that with his ex-perience he could handle it. It was for weekends only, a part-time job, at a higher wage, which meant he'd work less time and earn more money than at the Steak Out. He had talked it over with Tommy, who urged him to apply. Fred had offered to write him a letter of recommendation. He was pretty sure Mr. Farmer, the manager of the Steak Out, would put in a good word for him, since he knew about David's ambitions.

David was so nervous at his interview he thought he could not find his voice to speak to Mr. Martinez, the manager of the new place. He had with him a kind of résumé that he had con-cocted with the help of Tommy and Fred, describing his work in the kitchen at the Center and his job as salad boy and his plans to go to school to become a chef. Mr. Martinez, a stocky man with close-cropped hair and a pencil-line mustache, glanced at the paper without a word, folded it up, and handed it back to him.

"So you're at the Center?"

"Yes sir."

"You've been there how long?"

"Two years," David said. He explained that he was a Phase-Out now, and he would be graduating in a few months. He didn't know exactly how soon.

"That's the place for drug addicts and juvenile delinquents, and so on."

"Not exactly that. We've all had troubles, but we're learning to solve them there. It's a place where we've changed a lot."

"Don't bother with the public relations, son. I don't believe in any of that stuff. As far as I'm concerned, we all create our problems and we all dig our way out of them. If you want to show me that you can handle a job like this, then you cut out from that place and stand on your own two feet. If you're man enough to do that, the job is yours."

David was stunned, unable to believe what he had just heard. "You mean I can have the job if I leave the Center?"

"That's the deal."

"But it doesn't have anything to do with being a man, Mr. Martinez. I'm not going to leave the Center before I graduate. And I don't believe I'm interested in this job."

He had turned and left, aching more than he had in a long time.

"I'm still at the Steak Out," he told Tommy now. "Mr. Farmer said he might give me a raise."

"Hey, congratulations! And how about the girl? Heather?"

"Mostly I just see her at work."

"Have you asked her out yet?"

"Not yet."

"Jeez, Dave, when are you going to quit sitting on your thumbs and *do* something?"

Good question, and it came up in groups the same week.

"Hey, Peterson, what's the matter with you?" they challenged him. "You say you're lonely and you have trouble making friends. And there you are working at a place with nice, good-looking girls running all around and one of them even likes you enough to buy you a birthday cake and you still won't get off your ass. It's easier to feel sorry for yourself!"

Eventually he got up the nerve to take her home after work. He had planned to take her places, but he never quite got around to it. Someday he would take her to the movies and maybe for a hike or a picnic before it got too cold. Meanwhile, they talked on their breaks. He thought about her all the time, fantasizing about what they'd do on a real date, carrying on mental conversations with her, saving up little things to tell her when he saw her again. He thought he must be in love.

After work one night she invited him to a party. He was so surprised he hardly knew what to say. She was always surprising him, it seemed, but he was pleased. The party was much bigger than David had expected, and he didn't know most of the people there. There was some drinking, mostly beer and wine, and that made him even more nervous and ill at ease. Then he picked up the sweet smell of grass in the crowded room.

"Let's go," he said to Heather, taking her hand for the first time. "This is no place for me."

"Don't you ever get high?" she asked him. "I mean, you're almost a graduate now. What harm can it do you to smoke a joint once in a while? You don't have to be a pothead to have some fun now and then, do you?"

He stared at her, hoping the whole thing was a bad dream. "I don't get high, and I don't hang out with people who do. Let's go, Heather." He was almost pleading.

"But we just got here," she protested. "And I'm having a good time."

"I'm sorry, but I'm not. Are you coming with me?"

She tilted her head to one side, considering. "No," she said, "I guess I'm not." But she followed him out into the clear, cold night. There were stars and a big harvest moon; on the way to the party he had thought he'd probably kiss her later on under that moon. "I really like you and all," she was saying. "It's just that I like to get high once in a while. We'll still see each other, won't we?"

"I don't think so," he blurted out miserably. "No, I don't think we will."

He drove home slowly, wondering how he was going to handle this. He understood now why Tommy had had such a rough time as a Phase-Out.

The Phase-Out staff met in Dr. Stone's office, each carrying a stack of bulging files. Tommy Schwartz had David's. When he had first joined the staff, Tommy had spent a couple of hours a day in the examining room next to the nurse's office where the confidential files where kept on each client, reading carefully through the folder on each of the Phase-Outs, concentrating on his own cases but glancing at the others, too. Since he was involved with all of them in groups, this was the most efficient way to get the background on where the kids were coming from. If he had not been through it himself, he doubted that he would believe the changes they'd gone through. Flipping through the intake reports done by Dr. Stone or George, Tommy would have labeled many of them as losers with small chance of turning themselves around. And often, for a long time, not much progress seemed to be made, if you followed the monthly reports. Then, bit by bit, a pattern began to emerge. Never a straight line: apparent improvement and then some stupid backsliding, a hookup, a split, a return, a haircut, a job change, a leap forward, a fall back. An escalator, as David had said.

Tommy thumbed through David's file again. What a punky kid that one was! Had a jacket for lying, for sneakiness.

No punk any more, but he didn't seem very happy either. It was a tough thing for these kids; first you pull them in and get them to accept the Center as their whole world, not only their friends but their family too. And then you have to start pushing them out again. You have to teach them to fly. Some hang on too tight; others leap out of the nest before they're strong enough and fall hard and fast. Tommy had a vision of himself as a mother bird, nudging and encouraging but sometimes restraining. David was one of those birds who wasn't anxious to leave the nest.

The Phase-Out staff decided to give David a shove. He had been at the Center for over two years. No major problems in the last year. Slow in working his way through Intermediates, but going along pretty well as a Phase-Out. The usual problems of loneliness, finding a girlfriend, and so on. But keeping him in the program until the summer graduation rolled around probably wouldn't make him any stronger and might make him even more dependent. They decided that it was probably time for him to graduate but that they would continue to keep in close touch with him after he had gone.

"How's he doing at home?" Dr. Stone asked.

"Pretty good," Tommy reported. "He seems to have worked out some sort of relationship with his parents. He even managed to tell his father he loves him. Have you ever met that guy? Solid concrete. It must have really taken something for the kid to say that to his old man."

"What about the mother?"

"Okay, I guess. She and David are two of a kind—depressed and lonely and don't know what to do about it. But she's working and she seems to be holding together pretty well."

"No boyfriend in the picture, huh?"

"David hasn't mentioned one. I guess not."

"Just as well," Dr. Stone said. "Too many times the mother

moves a boyfriend into the house and then nobody gets along and there are jealousies all over the place."

"Lucky if it's only one boyfriend," George muttered. "Some of them have a regular parade."

"What about the brother and sister?"

"Both negatives, I'd say. The older brother took off some time ago. He was sort of the standard-bearer, following in the father's footsteps, and so on. Then he started getting high, I guess, and just began drifting. Pressures were too much for him, I suppose. He writes home for money once in a while, but that's about it. And the younger sister is definitely a problem. Dave has some guilt feelings about her, that maybe he's the cause of her getting into trouble. So far it's not too serious, but I wouldn't be terribly surprised if we have a second Peterson around here in the next year or so."

"Wouldn't be the first time we had a couple of kids from the same family," Dr. Stone said. "If only we could take the parents in the first place, we'd save everybody a lot of trouble and money."

"Shit," observed Charlie Toth, "if you could get to the parents in time you wouldn't have any kids here at all, and then we'd all be out looking for jobs."

George Miller leaped on that gleefully. "If we opened a therapeutic community for troubled parents, you could probably move half the country in here. I mean I would just *love* to hook some of those daddies up to the dishpan and put some of the mommies on the chair for a few days. Do them a world of good. Maybe they'd stop dumping their shit on their kids. You know, I walk into those Monday night Parents Group meetings, and there they are, so nice and respectable, until you sit through a session with them and all the garbage starts coming out."

"Yes, well, the new family counseling is going to help a lot. Some of the OR and Intermediate counselors are getting training in family systems therapy, so they'll be able to work from day one with the parents and other kids in the family. I wish we'd been able to start this years ago. It would have made a tremendous difference with somebody like Dave. Meanwhile, what are we going to do about him?"

"Put him through an evaluation and see what happens."

David was so nervous he could hardly knot his tie. He wondered who would be there, what kind of questions they were going to ask him, if he'd be able to answer the right way and still be honest. He kept asking himself the same thing the Phase-Out staff had been asking: Is David Peterson really ready to graduate?

David drove through a heavy downpour to the Center, parked the car in the muddy driveway and remembered to wipe his feet at the front door. It was not a regular Phase-Out meeting night, and there were a lot of people around whom he didn't know well. Even some ORs whose names he hadn't learned. They looked so sullen and sneaky. He wondered which ones among them would make it, which ones would split first. He had learned a long time ago that there wasn't any way to tell for sure. You just invested whatever you had and waited to see what happened. He had a lot of friends among the Intermediates though, and it still hurt when somebody with whom he had been tight split or fell. Never as bad as when Doug left, though. Since then he had learned that it might hurt unbearably, but you couldn't let it destroy you.

"Hey, Dave, what are you doing here tonight?"

"Evaluation."

Impressed, his friends backed away from him a little. It was the one thing that went on at the Center that was supposed to be kept secret. He didn't know quite what to expect, although Tommy had spent some time preparing him. There

172

would be people there to ask him questions. He didn't know exactly who. Sometimes people from the community were invited to an evaluation so they could get a better idea of what the Center was all about and so the person being evaluated would have another opportunity to talk about himself and his feelings in front of strangers. All he had to do was answer the questions.

That was all. His hands were clammy with sweat.

Tommy called him in. Dr. Stone was sitting at his big executive desk that was always so neat David had sometimes wondered just what it was a psychiatrist *did*, anyway. Dr. Stone waved him into the leather visitor's chair next to his desk, and David looked around nervously at the people seated in a semicircle facing him. Tommy, of course, but also Kevin and Betsy, and Charlie, the Phase-Out supervisor, and Paul Kendricks, and Mr. Anderson, the executive director of the Center, and Ms. Snyder, the woman who was writing the book. The office was stuffy, and Dr. Stone pushed open one of the windows. They listened to the rain splashing out of the gutter onto the stone terrace and dripping off the trees. Dr. Stone fiddled with a fancy letter opener and asked the first question.

"David, we'd like you to tell us about your life before you came to the Center."

He swallowed hard and described to them how unhappy he had been without quite knowing why. How he had started getting into trouble when he was about twelve, around the time he smoked his first reefer. How he started running around with a bunch of kids who were always getting high and then getting into trouble—stealing stuff, being truant from school, things like that. How he started doing all those things, too, just so he would have friends. How he fought with his parents. And how sick he felt inside but how he never told anybody how bad it was, not even himself.

"Tell us about your family."

He talked about his stern, distant father; his mother who always tried to shield him from his father; his older brother whom he idolized but at the same time hated because he believed his father loved him most; his pretty younger sister who was badly spoiled and seemed to be able to get away with practically anything. He told them how he resented all of this, and how he felt about the divorce, and how the resentment had gone away, and how much closer he felt to them now.

"So how did you feel when you first got here, Dave?"

"I kept saying to myself, 'I won't stay,' over and over, for days, maybe for weeks, and then I got a couple of friends." He recalled for them the first time he was able to open up in a group and how scared he was to let go. How afraid he was to care about anybody, and then about when he told Jay he loved him, and how hurt he had been when Doug split. So hurt that he left, and then came back.

It was sometime around then, he said—he wasn't exactly sure when it had been—that he realized how important the Center was to him. His own family was breaking up, and he was so sick and troubled by the divorce that he knew he would have come apart if he hadn't eventually learned that his life was right here. "I guess I finally understood that what I had to do was to change and become a man." A lump swelled unexpectedly in his throat. He wondered in panic if he was going to start to cry.

"How do you feel now about getting high? Do you think about it?"

He hesitated, relieved at the change in direction but not sure how to answer. The truth was that he still did think about it, and rather often. He sometimes yearned for the mellow feeling that always made everything seem right with the world. But should he tell them that? It would surely count against him. "Yes, I still think about it sometimes. But I wouldn't do it. I'm pretty sure about that." It was a shaky answer, but it was honest.

How would he feel about himself if he lied at his evaluation?

"How are you doing with girls, Dave? Have you been dating?"

Not much to say on this question. He saw Heather at work, and once in a while they talked a little. He still thought of her a lot, though, wondering if she was getting high regularly. But he hadn't talked to her about it, and he hadn't done anything at all about finding a new girl. He explained to them that he knew he had to get more aggressive about meeting girls and asking them out.

"What would you do if you met a girl you liked and you found out she gets high?"

"I wouldn't go out with her. That's what I found out about Heather, and so I stopped even talking to her about anything except work."

"But suppose you were really involved with her when you found out. What would you do then?"

Had he been really involved with Heather when he found out, at that party she had invited him to? In his head, maybe. "I'd try to talk her out of it," he said. "But I guess I probably wouldn't be able to, unless she cared more about me than she did about getting high. And if she wouldn't stop getting high, then I'd have to break off the relationship with her."

"Wouldn't that be pretty hard, Dave?"

"Yes, but I know for sure I'd do it. I know I'd have to, or it would be the end of me."

The next question was about morals, and he told them he hoped that if he did meet a girl he liked he'd be able to control himself and not try to talk her into having sex with him before they had developed some kind of relationship. He worried about that sometimes; when he was around girls it seemed that all he could think about was sex.

There were a lot of other questions, too: about his job,

about his plans for the future, about how he felt about the Center now. If he did get into trouble—got high, for example—would he be willing to come back to the Center for help? What would he do?

He thought that one over for a minute. "I'd be embarrassed," he confessed. "I'd feel like shit. But I think I'd come back." Then he added, "I know I would. Yes. I'd come back and ask for help."

One more thing: Did he have any criticisms of the Center? He scarcely hesitated. "I think you're getting too easy with some of the kids. They do something wrong, and all they get is a slap on the wrist. Things ought to be a lot tougher around here than they are." He didn't notice their smiles.

Then Paul Kendricks's gravelly voice cut in. "Dave, so far we've been asking all the questions, and you've been giving us the answers. Now it's your turn. Would you like to ask any of us anything?"

He hadn't expected that. He turned to Kevin, the one with whom he still felt most closely involved. So close he didn't even have to ask the question. Kevin shook a cigarette from the pack in his shirt pocket, lit it, and handed it to David.

"I was never sure we were going to be able to keep you, Dave. You were such a hard person to reach. There were times when I thought what you needed more than anything I could ever say to you was a good kick in the ass. And when you pulled that stupid trick when Doug left, I just figured we had lost you for good. And I wondered what was ever going to knock some sense into that thick head of yours."

"Stubborn!" Betsy added. "And clever. Sneaky-clever. We'd think you were making progress and then wham, back to zero again. After a while it does make you wonder."

They reminded him of his General Meeting, of his haircut, of his endless hookups.

"But listen, Dave," Kevin said in a voice huskier than David was used to, "I want you to know something. I love you. I really love you, man."

"Me too, Dave," Betsy said.

The last of David's reserves dwindled to nothing. The lump in his throat exploded, and he began to cry, the tears running unchecked. The one that got him finally, he guessed, was Betsy. She had never told him before that she loved him. She once had said, "You know I do. Why must I say it?" But now she had said it, too, and he could feel the affection and warmth in the room wrap itself around him.

He went to each of them, including Ms. Snyder, whose face was wet, too, and held them tight in an embrace meant to convey everything he felt. They had helped him choose to live. No matter what happened in the years ahead, David knew that this was really where his life had begun.

CHAPTER 8

IT WAS THE NIGHT OF GRADUATION, AND DAVID LOOKED AND felt terrific. He had had his hair cut for the occasion, and his father had bought him a splendid gray pinstripe suit with a vest. He and the other graduates had seats in the front of the auditorium. The rest of the family from the Center sat behind him, and their friends and relatives filled in the rows toward the back.

On the stage, looking strangely dressed up, were the counselors and the high rollers, along with a number of people David had seen only at graduations, like the chairman of the board of directors. Mr. Alderson, the executive director, was up there, too, and a priest and a minister to say the prayers, plus a guy who was going to make a speech. David hoped it would be a short one.

Mr. Alderson got things started right on time and they moved quickly through the formalities, the invocation, the national anthem played on a tinny piano, and then Carla MacLoughlin, looking poised and pretty in a long white dress with a blue shawl, recited the Philosophy. George Miller, gold watch chain flashing, introduced the staff, and as each one rose to acknowledge the introduction, the family applauded, stamping and clapping loudly for the people they were close to.

The only tense moment of the ceremony was Paul Kendricks's announcement of the new group of Phase-Outs. David knew how some of the older Intermediates felt. Paul read the names, allowing time between each one for the ecstatic response of the new Phase-Out and the enthusiasm of his friends, and playing his usual graduation-night joke of "forgetting" one name and coming back to the microphone to correct the omission. David joined in the congratulations, of course, glad that some of his friends were making it, but he didn't feel the way he used to. He had begun to move away from all of it.

The presentation of graduates was a more formal affair. One by one as their names were called, they walked up to the stage to receive a diploma from the chairman of the board and the good wishes of the staff.

"David Peterson."

He rose, unconsciously straightened his tie, and strode confidently toward the stage.

\* \* \*

Sitting toward the back of the auditorium with Susie between them, Ellen Kucera Peterson and Richard Peterson watched their son cross the stage. Richard gazed in wonder at David, now fully six feet tall and a couple of inches bigger than his father, handsome in his new suit, that brown hair longer than he really liked to see it on a boy but neat and shining. He watched his son cross the stage and shake the chairman's hand and accept his diploma, and Richard clenched his jaws hard to fight back the tears.

Ellen didn't bother to restrain them. She could hardly believe that the self-confident young man making his way across the stage to hug Paul Kendricks was the same sullen boy who had made them all so miserable a couple of years ago that she thought she would never survive the pain. Everything in her life had changed since then. She wasn't sure if most of it was for the better or not. But this certainly was. What had happened to David was nothing sort of a miracle.

Ellen and Richard exchanged glances over Susie's head and nodded mutely. Their boy had made it.

Standing up to greet the big kid with the exultant grin, Kevin Murphy was not thinking in terms of miracles. He had been to quite a few of these graduations, including his own, and he hardly ever got through it dry-eyed. It was not a miracle. It was damned hard work for every person on the stage as well as for the people sitting out front. There was scarcely anyone here who had not given up a lot of his own time and certainly more energy than he had ever thought possible, as well as a tremendous amount of love. But it all came back to you at times like this—seeing these kids, such tattered and beaten scraps of humanity when they had first come to the Center, who by tremendous effort had turned themselves into fully formed human beings. He hugged David, nearly knocked off-balance by the tall boy's strength and enthusiasm.

Then he watched David hug Betsy more gently. Kevin and Betsy were getting married in three weeks, the day after Christmas. They had invited all the kids from the Center as their guests. Kevin was still marveling that they were actually going to do it. It hadn't been easy. They had even split up once, somehow carrying on their duties at the Center without telegraphing their problems to everybody else. That hadn't been easy, either. Kevin caught Betsy's eye and winked. Their boy had made it.

David Peterson is not a real name or an actual person, but he is certainly typical of the kind of boy who might have found himself at the Center and made his slow, struggling way through the program. The Center is real enough, however, a somewhat fictionalized version of Vitam Center in Norwalk, Connecticut.

Vitam (pronounced VEE-tom) takes its name from its Latin motto, ERGO LEGE VITAM, quoting part of the Old Testament verse, "I call heaven and earth to record . . . that I have set before you life and death, blessing and curse, *therefore choose life*, that thou and thy seed may live." (Deuteronomy, 30:19) It's a place where teen-agers with troubles—emotional problems as well as problems with drugs, school, parents, the law—learn how to change.

Vitam is a therapeutic community, a group of people living together for the purpose of helping themselves and each other to deal with the problems that overwhelm them. There are a number of therapeutic communities of different types that deal with different kinds of people and situations, perhaps well over two hundred of them in the United States, based on the idea developed in the 1930s in England that disturbed people should take an active role in their own treatment. The popular idea then (and the one still best known today) is that an expert, such as a psychiatrist, administers the cure to a patient, seen as someone who is unable to help himself. But in the therapeutic community, everybody helps everybody else: "You alone can do it, but you can't do it alone." Because the people at Vitam are young, there are older "helping people" acting as counselors, many of whom have themselves been through Vitam or programs like it.

One of the oldest programs in which members help themselves by helping each other is Alcoholics Anonymous, founded in the United States in 1935 to assist people suffering from alcoholism to stop drinking. Then, in the 1960s, when addiction to heroin became a serious problem among adults, especially the younger ones, various therapeutic communities arose, modeled on some of the principles of Alcoholics Anonymous. In programs such as Daytop, Phoenix House, Odyssey House, and others, addicts lived together in a community to support each other's efforts to kick the habit that was ruining their lives. Many of the terms and techniques utilized by such programs— haircuts, morning meetings, the encounter groups in which members confront each other—have been adapted for use at Vitam. The techniques have been modified and new ones added because the adolescents who come to the Center today for treatment are so much younger than the addicts who found help at the older therapeutic communities, and heroin has practically disappeared as a problem among Vitam's clientele.

Known as "clients" rather than "patients" in their records, referred to by the staff as "kids," and called "members" by each other, most of the boys and girls at Vitam are between thirteen and eighteen; a few are older and one or two even younger; the average age, now fifteen, has been dropping steadily. Boys outnumber girls nearly three to one, but the percentage of girls is increasing. The majority are from the Fairfield County, Connecticut, area, and most of the others come from other Connecticut towns, with a few from other parts of the country. Most are from middle-class families; less than one-third are from poverty-level families, and some have upper-class backgrounds. The ethnic mix is roughly eighty-eight percent white, six percent black and six percent Hispanic.

More than half the clients at Vitam are sent there by the courts or by probation officers. A quarter come because their parents bring them, and the rest are referred by counselors, doctors, lawyers and clergymen. For those who come through court referral, Vitam is but one option: there are other state-operated facilities where they can be sent, for however long the judge decides. In most of these places the person simply serves time. At Vitam he has the challenge and the possibility of dramatic change.

The idea that would eventually evolve into the Vitam Center had its beginning in the mid-1960s, about the time people were becoming increasingly aware of the growing use of drugs by teen-agers. It was no longer something that happened to somebody else's kids in an ugly slum in some other city. It was happening right there in affluent Fairfield County, where drugs were easily available in the hallways of the sleek modern suburban schools.

Nobody quite knew the extent of the drug problem. There were few ideas for handling it, virtually no facilities, and scarcely any public funds. But there was Dr. Walter X. Lehmann, a pediatrician in Wilton, Connecticut, who had been working with young people in his office, on his own time, and sometimes in his own home, on problems of drug addiction that usually involved emotional problems as well. And there was a group of concerned citizens in the area. The group and the doctor joined forces in the late sixties and established the John J.

Hooper Youth Foundation, named for the Jesuit priest who sent the first troubled kid to Dr. Lehmann for help.

In 1970 a treatment center was set up in a former private school and given its name: VITAM. The staff included five people: Dr. Lehmann, a registered nurse, and three ex-addict therapists. The demand for services far outstripped Vitam's operating capacity. It was obvious that while some people could get the help they needed staying at home but spending most of their time at Vitam, many desperately needed a place to live, both to get them away from the negative influences of their home environment and to increase the pressure on them to change. In 1972, only nine people could be housed at Vitam, but within a couple of years facilities were expanded to accommodate forty boys. A wing added to the Main Building increased the facilities, and renovation of the third floor provided dormitory space for sixteen girls. A new building program launched in 1977 will substantially increase Vitam's capacity, still keeping the number of clients at a level that can be handled without sacrificing treatment quality within the concept of a therapeutic "family."

Meanwhile, nothing stands still at Vitam. A group home has been set up for graduates with no place to go, one of the few group homes in the state for both boys and girls. The vital Family Counseling Services program is helping whole families to change and grow. There have been additions to the school curriculum, a bus has replaced the van, even the muddy driveway in which Betsy's car bogged down has been blacktopped, and the changes continue.

In the 1960s, when Dr. Lehmann first began working with drug abuse cases, his patients were heroin addicts in their late teens and early twenties. But by 1972, the age of the people coming to Vitam had begun to drop, and most of the clients were experimenting with several drugs. Four years later most of Vitam's population was under eighteen, the average fifteen.

Most of them used marijuana and alcohol, with a substantial percentage using barbiturates, amphetamines, and hallucinogens. Very few, if any, were using heroin. Unlike the heroin addicts who came to Vitam with the intention of breaking the habit, most of the recent arrivals today have little motivation to quit but are sent there by *other people* who want them to quit. The peer pressure on the "outside" to continue drug use is enormous. Most of the new Vitam clients have severe emotional and developmental problems.

Treatment methods for younger clients are more complicated and demanding than they were for older Vitam clients. A less rigid program structure, a warmer atmosphere, and a modification of the hard-hitting encounter techniques that were the earmark of older therapeutic communities all had to be developed. The old staff had to learn new techniques, and more professionally trained people were required. Dr. Lehmann retired from Vitam in 1976 after years of selfless work. The Vitam team now includes a psychiatrist, a clinical psychologist, social workers, and experienced, skilled counselors. There is also a pediatrician and three nurses, as well as an education director to supervise the fully staffed Vitam School, which specializes in handling learning disabilities.

Like David Peterson, the people who come to Vitam need to feel that someone really cares. A new member first becomes part of a stable family group (if he stays; nearly a third leave in the first month, and the first three months of Orientation are crucial). In this controlled environment the member slowly learns a new way to live—without drugs, without getting into trouble. Gradually he assumes responsibility in amounts that increase as he learns to handle it. Then he starts to look deeper into himself, unlocking his inner feelings, learning to deal with them, discovering how he is seen by others and how he must deal with others on an emotional level.

The techniques that make this happen are a combination of individual psychotherapy—David's long talks with Kevin or Betsy or Tommy—and encounter groups in which he is confronted by his peers on his behavior and encouraged to talk about his feelings.

Vitam's therapy emphasizes moral values, the recognition of right and wrong, the responsibility of the individual for making correct choices and accepting the outcome of his actions. Drawing on the techniques of reality therapy, an approach developed by California psychiatrist William Glasser, also emphasizes the emotional involvement of the helping person with the person being helped. Unlike more traditional methods of treating emotional problems, reality therapy is not concerned with the person's past but with his present and his future. People involved in reality therapy learn to fulfill their needs in ways that don't deprive others of fulfillment of *their* needs.

The other side of caring is discipline, and Vitam is known for its toughness. Outsiders accustomed to therapy techniques that emphasize a kindly sort of ego reinforcement as a way of building self-esteem are shocked and sometimes dismayed at the yelling, the verbal abuse, the bad language, and wonder if that isn't going to crush an already damaged personality. Vitam's answer is no; the toughness is never beyond the individual's ability to cope with it, and it's far more effective in bringing about changes in personality than a pat on the head when the person's counselor and his peers and the person himself all know the pat is undeserved.

Vitam's methods work, though not for everyone. More than three hundred people have graduated from the program. About fifteen hundred teen-agers have been seen by the staff since Vitam opened its doors in July 1970; about half of them were admitted to the program, and fewer than half of those admitted made it all the way through to graduation.

There are stories of people who stayed for only a few weeks and then left but continued to improve dramatically on their own. There are also stories of members who came within weeks of graduation, split, never came back and soon reverted to their old ways. There are stories, too, of people who graduated and then fell soon after graduation, unable to make it on their own. But not all of them remained "fallen"; some went through a difficult period and then sought more help or were able to straighten themselves out on their own. And of course there are some graduates who fall and do eventually go back to a negative lifestyle, forming detrimental relationships, getting high, and finding themselves in trouble with the law all over again.

A few years ago a study was made of the 203 people who had graduated from Vitam from 1971 through 1975. Of these, 157—78 percent—were counted as "successfully rehabilitated"; they had continued to be drug-free and well adjusted, had jobs or were getting along successfully, had developed positive relationships and were in general "doing well"; some had had temporary setbacks, but had then straightened out, either alone or with further help and were continuing to progress. Twenty-six of the 203 were considered "unsuccessful," and twenty others were "unknown." A similar study done in 1978 on more recent graduates showed the same proportion of success, about eighty percent.

The trick is to keep a client in the program for just the right amount of time. If he doesn't stay long enough, he won't have fully internalized all the values and controls he's been learning, and under the harsh realities and relentless pressures of the outside world, he's likely to cave in. For that reason, the average amount of time spent in the program has increased from its early days. It used to be from six to eighteen months; today two years or longer is usual.

If a member stays too long, however, there is always the

danger that he may become institutionalized, too dependent on the strong and artificial environment of Vitam.

Younger clients are easier to help, but they are also sent back out into the world at a vulnerable age, some still in the midst of their tumultuous adolescent years and the older ones as yet under the legal age for learning to handle alcoholic beverages in moderation. (Although they will never be permitted to use drugs, not even marijuana should it be legalized, they are, at the age of eighteen, allowed to drink a beer or two.)

There is no way of telling what lies in the future of any Vitam graduate, as there is no way of predicting with certainty what will happen to any young person on the threshold of adulthood. Some models of success are right there at Vitam where several staff members (counselor-therapists and high rollers, too) are themselves graduates of the program. And every graduate has said or listened to the Vitam Philosophy hundreds of times, until it has been engraved on his heart:

*Seeking an end to our troubles, we have, in our own ways, begun here. We discover that our past is left behind only when we begin new lives. Alone we have failed; together we can choose to live.*

*Let us then be honest with one another;*

*Let us trust one another;*

*Let there be a feeling of concern among us, one for the other;*

*Let there be a common commitment toward personal growth and the growth of the Vitam family as a whole;*

*Above all, let us be unafraid to love one another.*

It's all true for David. The graduation address, mercifully short, was followed by the benediction, and then everyone adjourned for a party in the cafeteria. There was a big crowd, and flashbulbs were popping everywhere. David found his mother and father, together even if they were not looking at each other and were keeping Susie between them. David could tell they'd been crying. He hugged all three of them. His father's body was tense as he exercised self-control. Susie grinned self-consciously and accepted the hug passively. His mother embraced him fiercely and then ducked away, using her own way to hold herself together. She had to go help with the food. Betsy and Kevin and some of the other staff stopped to say hello to the Petersons, and David introduced some of his friends.

The tables were nearly overflowing with cakes, cookies, fruit, cheese, and other good food brought in by the parents, but David was almost too excited to eat. Everybody seemed happy, except for the usual few who had thought they would make Phase-Out and hadn't. David remembered when he had felt that way. He looked around for some of the other graduates and spotted Pete Barlow and Eddie Simmons in the crowd. There were sixteen of them, and Pete's parents had invited them over to their big house for a party afterwards. Actually the celebration would split into two parties; those over eighteen would go out together to a bar later for a couple of beers, and the rest would stick with soft drinks and pizza and lots of loud music at the Barlows'. Carla would be there. Now that they were graduates they were free to date, but it had taken David a long time to regard her as a sister, and now he was not sure he could get past those feelings and relate to her on a different level.

Then he spotted Heather. She was standing off by herself, away from the crowd and looking a little lost. He had kept his distance from her for months, talking with her at the restaurant and being pleasant and friendly but trying not to be around her. There had been times when he thought he couldn't stand it. She was so pretty, so nice, so friendly. But she got high, he knew that, and he had to stay away.

So what was she doing at graduation? She had heard him

talk about it, but she had never said anything about coming. Maybe she had come for somebody else; it must be. But who? There was no reason she would come for him. Still, every time he glanced her way, she was looking at him with a little smile. Finally, when he had greeted everybody and seemed to be alone for a minute, she came over to him and held out her hand.

"Congratulations," she said.

"Thanks." He felt awkward. "What are you doing here?" he asked, not very diplomatically.

"I guess I just wanted to see you graduate."

"*Me?*"

She nodded. "I don't get high any more," she said, almost whispering. "I kept thinking about some of the things you said, and I got to see how dumb it was."

He could hardly believe it. He thought his ears were doing strange things, but finally he got it together. "I'm glad," he managed to say. Then he made a decision. "Because I'd like to take you to the movies next weekend, if you'd like to go."

She said she would. He grinned and said he'd see her at work, but now he had to go. He explained about the graduates' party. He thanked her for coming and shook her hand and thought that this weekend he was going to be with her. Maybe he'd even kiss her. He had never felt better in his life.

In the summer of 1977 Carolyn Meyer had two house-guests: her son, John, who had been in the Vitam program for one year, and his friend, Jimmy. It was not an easy visit, partly due to family circumstances in the aftermath of divorce, and partly because it seemed to her that John and Jimmy were speaking in a different language about a different world. In an effort to relate to the boys, Meyer the Writer as well as Carolyn the Mother brought out a notebook and began to jot down some of the things they were talking about. It was a valid technique; she began to comprehend their world, and she had an idea for a new book.

Within a few months she had approval from Vitam Center to begin research. During the winter of 1977 and through the first part of 1978, she spent a few days each week at the Center, getting acquainted first with the staff and then with the boys and girls. She ate with them, sat in groups with them, rapped with them in the living room, observed them in the classroom, and helped cook Christmas dinner for them.

In the process an odd thing happened. What had begun as a research project for a book became an intense emotional involvement. She began to relax around the staff and to enjoy their company on a personal level. And she began to care enormously about the boys and girls with whom she was spending time. She found that her hours at the Center had become the most valuable in her week. She memorized the Vitam Philosophy in case anyone might call on her at a meeting to recite it (no one did). And she found herself growing closer to her son after months of pain and separation.

March 23, 1978, was to be her last day at Vitam. Then she was to go off and write the book. John's primary counselor suggested that she stay around for the big house meeting that night. She guessed what was going to happen and would not have missed it for anything. It had been agreed that through the weeks of research she would avoid all of the encounter groups in which John was taking part; she would have inhibited him, certainly, and she knew she could not have stood the raw emotion of seeing her son in those circumstances. In the big meetings she stayed on the other side of the room, out of his range of vision. But on that March night, she sat down next to him.

First the medical director, Dr. Norman Levy, made a little farewell speech to Carolyn, who had become part of the family. Everybody clapped. Carolyn responded with a few words about serendipity, about how she had come looking for one thing and found something of even greater importance. She thanked the staff and acknowledged the person who was most important in the research: her son, John. John looked embarrassed and pleased.

The main purpose of the meeting was to announce the new Phase-Outs. Carolyn looked at John, whose name had been at the top of the Intermediate pop-sheet for months. "My heart's pounding," he whispered. John's counselor stood up to make the first announcement. Carolyn felt as though her lungs would explode, and she could see John's facial muscles tensing. "This person has been in the program for a long time, and I've seen him go through a million changes. He happens to be sitting next to his mother."

John sprang up with a joyous yell. Carolyn, not at all surprised, promptly burst into tears anyway. The son hugged his mother, and his mother hugged him back.